The Witching Woods

Iris Mann

Published by Trellis Publishing, 2021.

This is a work of fiction. Similarities to real people, places, or events are entirely coincidental.

THE WITCHING WOODS

First edition. July 15, 2021.

Copyright © 2021 Iris Mann.

ISBN: 979-8224900176

Written by Iris Mann.

THE WITCHING WOODS

IRIS MANN

With a name like "Salem Wood Academy for Young Girls," it appeared exactly as you'd expect, one-part aged and antique, the other eerie and haunting. Everything from the old windows stained with the fumes of candles decades since burned to the stout door frames, hand made many years ago, to the old family cemetery behind the main hall, the one everyone swore was haunted, spoke of another time cloaked in mystery and betrayal. Why Jane's mother had decided she was to stay here instead of a local, public school, she still could not tell. But as she rode the all but empty bus up the cobblestone road though the enormous, decorative gate, she couldn't help but feel like it was some sort of punishment.

She was welcomed with the old, dressed in a clean but clearly over worn uniform and presented to an uptight, pursed-lipped woman who was introduced as Headmistress Buckland.

"Miss Saxon, I presume?"

"Yes, Ma'am," Jane gave a slight courtesy, not knowing what was customary.

But the lady seemed pleased, "Good. Follow me dear, if you would," she tapped through the old corridors of the old hall like a dressage horse, her head barely bobbing as she stepped, "We hope you will find this place a home while you are here. But do not forget you are here to learn discipline, courtesy, and respect, not to experiment with unsavory pastimes or spend your days fraternizing. Understood?"

"Understood."

"Good. And it will serve you well to project your speech and look up from your shoes." How she had noticed, Jane had no idea, she was facing straight forward as she spoke, "Now this is the main hall where you may find the staff should a situation arise, though I trust you would strive to stay far away from people who may cause such trouble." What trouble she spoke up Jane also had no clue. Were there arsonists and junkies housed here, or was reading anything other than the Bible still an offense in this city?

Either way, she would soon find out as after the brief tour through the small campus (under the assurance that the other girls would show her everything else she needed), she was lead to the dormitory, a building as old and historical as all the others.

The headmistress strode to the base of the stairs of the winding abode, portraits of the headmistresses she had succeeded watching her with her same brand of tight-lipped, eye piercing judgment. She rung a small bell at the base of the stairs and took a step back. Within moments a collection of about thirty girls rushed down the stairs and aligned themselves on the landing, "Girls, pay attention," she instructed as the beating of feet began to hush, "This is Miss Jane Saxon, your new class and dorm mate. She is joining us a few months late as you know, but I would like you all to get her properly initiated and prepared for fall quarter when it begins. She will be staying in room 211 so you four," she clapped her hands as if she was trying to light a Clap On, "help her carry her things and show her to her bed."

The rest of the girls took this as a cue to leave and disappeared back to their rooms with a curtsy, some very tight and proper, others far less so. But four girls stepped forth, one looking welcoming and bright-eyed, the other three looking positively disdainful.

"This is Miss Abbot, Miss Black, Miss Archer, and Miss Hale." The all curtseyed again, but very slightly,"

"Pleased to meet you," said the friendly looking one, the one introduced as Miss Archer. Jane just nodded.

"The customs, the schedule, the map of campus: I want you all to teach her post haste. Can you do that?"

"Consider it done, ma'am." Archer chirped again.

"Very good. Then I will see you ladies at supper." And she trotted off the way she came.

As soon as the great doors had closed behind her, the three other girls all picked up something menial and went back to the room without much more than a scoff. Archer, on the other hand, picked up her entire suitcase and held out a hand, "Hi, I'm Lucy," she said, still sincerely happily.

"Jane. But you knew that."

'Yeah. But that's Sarah, Grace, and Edith. They probably aren't going to talk to you too much. Just ignore them; that's what I do."

They began up the stairs, creaky but not chipped or in the slightest bit dusty. She gazed around at the paintings on the walls and carvings on the handrails, "So what all do I have to learn?'

"Oh it's not too much," she grunted as she lugged the luggage up the final step, "We have breakfast at six-thirty, luncheon at one, and supper at seven. Except weekends we only have brunch at eleven. Oh, and they do take attendance so you have to come. Cleaning is every Sunday morning and they inspect while we're at breakfast. Let's see, always say 'yes ma'am, no ma'am, right away, ma'am.' Curtsey mean's hello and goodbye. I'll give you the tour tomorrow and everything else you should be able to work out as you go." She nudged open the door that was already ajar, the one with '211' carved in the glossy wood. Dust and grime wise it was immaculately clean but otherwise there were clothes, bags, books, and all sorts of things strewn across the floors and beds which there were six of. Despite this, it seemed quite a cozy place. It was at the very least the only place with anything that could be called modern. There did not seem to be any electricity, however. The other girls scowled at Jane as she came in the door but soon returned to the tight circle they were sitting in hovering over...something, "Well, here we are. Home, sweet home. Here, why don't you take this bed?"

"Hey, what are you doing with that?" One of the girls snapped.

"Giving it to Jane. You know, the new girl you didn't even bother to say hello to?"

"Her bed's over there," she pointed to a bed in the corner with her three tiny bags placed haphazardly on it.

"You know there's a spring poking out of that one."

"Well I'm sorry, but this one's mine."

"Just because you pile your stuff on it doesn't make it yours. Besides, there's only three of you, you don't need four beds."

She groaned, "Fine. But as soon as she's gone it's mine again." She removed her pile of things in a huff and dumped them beside her actual bed. Jane and Lucy carried the bed to the other side of the room near Lucy's bed, just below the window. She got a desk as well with an old chair and a pleasant view of the stables.

By the time she had unpacked all of her things, it was already supper time and they all hurried to the dining hall. The food was dry and bland and it seems the girls who cooked it had been told as much and were sulking in their table by the kitchen. Lucy had introduced Jane to some other very nice and friendly girls who could not help but blather on how much they loved horse riding and how much Jane would love it. She slowly began to believe this wasn't just a place for girls who needed discipline but also for girls who enjoyed it.

However, she could not help but notice Sarah, Grace, and Edith in their own edge of one of the long tables, a chair or two between them and the other students as if a wicked, black aura were pushing them away.

Or maybe it was just their cattiness.

Back at the dorm, she went back to what she loved doing most, reading. She loved stories of mystery and adventure, something she felt she would be sorely lacking in this high-strung place. But as she got a few pages deeper into her latest tale, the three girls arose from their private corner like a flock of harpies.

Grace thrust a card in her face, "Is this you?" Jane lifted her glasses to read it. It was a tarot card, The Tower to be exact.

"I don't know. I haven't decided."

"That so? Who are you planning on destroying exactly? Us?"

"Are you that special?" Grace scoffed in disbelief, "Besides the tower doesn't always mean destruction. It can mean upheaval or great change."

"In that case, you better still lay off because we like things exactly as they are. Got it?"

"Hey, Hecate," Lucy grumbled from her desk where she was writing, "I think your cauldron's double, double bubbling over. Go cause some toil and trouble somewhere else."

"This doesn't concern you. I'd stay away from this abomination if you want to be free of the turmoil that will follow her."

"Thanks for the advice. Now run along, your flying monkeys need feeding." They all returned to their corner, but not without a scornful stare.

"Flying monkeys?" Jane looked back with a smile.

"I got a million of them," Lucy winked.

Lucy had failed to mention that there was a lights out time at nine. But it was then when everyone had gone to bed, there was heavy, sleep enraptured breathing coming from every bed, that Jane slid her book off of the desk slunk under the covers and whispered a short spell. With a flick of her fingers, a warm, orange ball of light was sprung into being. She read by the magical light long into the cold night.

As promised, Lucy took her on a tour the next morning. After breakfast she walked her to the horse stables and showed her the many horses, some already being ridden around the tracks and fields. Then there was the art gallery. It was actually quite something to see, better than almost anything she had seen displayed at a public school. Then again, they had a hundred years of legacy populating the shelves; they probably did not keep the bad stuff.

As they wandered over to the auditorium, they bumped into their roommates, walking around the garden, collecting flowers it seemed, "What is their deal, exactly?"

"They think they're witches," Lucy said rolling her eyes, "They do their readings, make their potions, cast spells, that kind of thing. It's all the time too, I swear."

"They cast spells? Like what?"

"I don't know. They don't tell me, of course. But they seem to do it whenever anything happens, like a spell of luck during exams, a spell to make the snow fall harder so classes get canceled, that type of thing. Oh, and sometimes they hex people."

"Hex people? Does it work?"

"Of course not," she seemed surprised Jane would even ask.

"But then why does everyone seem so afraid of them?"

"Well, okay, there was one thing that happened last year," she walked closer to Jane and spoke in a low voice, "We don't like to talk about it but it's best you know. Last year a girl went up to the top of the tower in the main hall and jumped. No one knew why she did it but it was...terrible." She shuddered, "Anyway, the thing is the witch girls hated her for some reason. They said she was 'malificarum,' whatever that means. They bullied her, tried to get her expelled, and then apparently they hexed her. But, you know, magic isn't real like that. My guess is she just had enough." They walked in silence for a while until they finally reached the auditorium, "You spooked enough yet? They say this place is haunted." She shook her head again in disbelief and disappointment.

Unlike the gallery and stables, this building was empty. All the lights were off and it was still cold from the autumn night's cold air. Lucy pointed out the boxes, the backstage, the walkways, the light room, and the props room which Jane was, for some reason she could not describe, drawn to.

"You mind if I take a look around?"

"No problem. You like costumes?"

Jane nodded. There were many in here and they all seemed remarkably detailed, some even authentic, nothing like the twenty dollar Halloween garb she was accustomed to. The props too were quite something: hand painted set pieces, wood carved canes and weapons, and classic, old furniture. It smelled like velvet and dust and it was wonderful.

And then she saw something she did not expect: a boy.

"H-hello?"

"Oh, hello." He said. He was dressed as a farm boy with tangled dark hair and sun-ravaged skin, "Are they...is it...over?"

"Is what over?"

He got up and ran to a nearby antique mirror, only to see that he had no reflection. He sighed, somehow not surprised, "Are you...you must be a witch then."

"Me? No. I mean, at least, not really."

"You must be. How else could you see me?"

"Jane? Are you back there?" she flinched at the sound of Lucy's voice.

"I have to go."

"No, please!" he lurched forward, the low light casting harsh shadows on his face, "Please, don't leave. It's been so long."

"Here, how about I come back?"

"You'll forget. They always forget."

"I won't." the boy didn't look so sure, "Here, I'll write It down." She went into her school bag and opened her notebook to the day's date and wrote in a reminder, "See?"

"There you are," She flipped around to see Jane, "I thought you'd gotten lost. Who were you talking to?"

She turned back to see no one. The boy, whoever or whatever he was, had vanished, "Oh, just myself. Wonderful costumes."

"Aren't they? Now we'd better hurry. It's almost time for lunch."

She nodded. Before she left, she looked back once more. Nothing.

On their walk back from luncheon, Lucy showed her an alternate path, a scenic route through the gardens. There were gorgeous flowers, babbling brooks, and several statues. However, at one she stopped dead in her tracks.

"Emma?" she whispered.

Lucy stopped, "Oh yeah, that's Emma Lamb, the one who killed herself."

"She's my cousin," her eyes were empty.

"She was? Why didn't you tell me?"

"I didn't know. I didn't know she went here. I didn't know that's how she…"

Lucy put a gentle hand on her shoulder, "I'm so sorry. If you need—"

"I knew it," Sarah, tailed by her fellow witches, was suddenly upon them, "And you're just like her too." She smirked ever so slightly, "Malificarum," she whispered.

And they left just as quickly as they had come.

Jane suddenly realized that her heart was racing, her breathing heavy, "Hey, can we go somewhere quiet? Not the room." Lucy nodded and lead her toward the library.

For a while, she had just cried. Lucy did not disturb her as it seemed to be what she wanted and the few others in there paid her no mind.

How could she live in this place? she thought. As an only child, her cousin Emma had been a sister to her, sharing her interests, comforting her on bad days and creating the good ones. She had just disappeared one day for a school somewhere for some reason that she was never told. The loneliness that followed was gloomy and she longed for the return of her best friend. She thought it would be soon, that hopefully, she would be back by summer. Yet in the early spring, she was told that Emma had died. She knew it was a suicide but little else. When she realized the loneliness would be forever, she sunk into a bleak sadness.

Because not only did they share their interests and their sense of humor, but they shared something more special: magic. Ever since they were young children, they knew they were gifted with something. They could move things without touching them, summon light and the wind, even briefly turn invisible. It was something they practiced at sleepovers and trips into the shaded parks near their houses. It was something wonderful that they shared, something that they alone had together. When she died, so did it. She hardly practiced her magic since then.

And now she would be living with the girls who took her away. Whether it was through magic or harassment, it didn't matter.

Some emotion between vengeance, sadness, and anger compelled Jane to wipe the tears from her face, stand, and walk through the library halls. She was looking for the local history books. This being Salem, there was, of course, plenty on witchcraft and the witch trials. She was looking through the books for one word in particular: "maleficarum." While there was no record of the word alone, there were a few mentions of another book, one called Malleus Maleficarum or Hammer of Witches. It was a very old witch-hunting book that was written over two centuries before the witch trials yet it seemed to be referenced for determining whether one was a witch and how to kill said witches. The book itself wasn't in the library but there were others on the subject. She picked up half a dozen history and witch hunting books and checked them out of the library and tucked them safely away in her bag where no one else could see it.

Lucy, before she had left while Jane was still crying, had said that she would be in the dorm, ready to protect her from the witch girls and whatever nastiness they might inflict on her. Indeed, when she returned, the girls were keeping to themselves, glancing up but not staring like before. Even still, Jane could not help from sickening feeling a crawling up her back. Even with all her books, she desperately wanted to get lost in her storybook and read it until dinner.

When she returned, she poured through the books. There was much of this place's history, and what a grim past it was. However, most of the writers were of the belief that everything regarding witchcraft was false, just something to condemn the unwanted, and that actual witchcraft did not exist. What she did find was that all the books that did cite magic as a real possibility spoke of events long after the witch trials. It told of a feud between two covens of self-proclaimed witches who fought each other mercilessly in the shadows. They were said to be born and destined to be rivals of one another, rivals who would fight until their enemies were destroyed.

And then, according to all accounts, both witch families were destroyed.

She was writing in her notebook all of the little notes she came across, starring and underlining the most important hints. Then as she turned a page, she saw a message, one she did not remember writing: Meet the boy in the costume closet. What it meant, she didn't know. Was it a hint or a trap? She had remembered being in the costume closet, marveling at the old attire. And then the memory was hazy as if someone had cut out and stitched up her memory, removing something completely. She could see hints of what it was along the seam. She must have written this herself, it was in her handwriting. She decided she had to go.

She could not quite believe herself—the first week at a boarding school meant to teach discipline and she was sneaking out in the middle of the night to follow some mysterious note. Luckily for her, her roommates seemed like they were under a sleeping curse every night so sneaking away was a breeze. The main door had an alarm set once the lights were out. However, there was an old fire escape that ironically was not alarmed and was nearby her room on the second floor. When she hit solid earth in the gardens below, she headed toward the woods, on the outskirts of which was where the theater was nested.

The front door was locked. The side door was locked. Every window, panel, and vent were locked up as tight as a prison. She walked around the back and there was almost nothing there. Almost. For at the very bottom hidden by a bramble of bushed was a cellar door, the chain lock broken to pieces. She heaved up the heavy door and it closed behind her with a clang. She prayed it had not awakened anything I these dreadfully deep, dark woods.

It was pitch black in here as well so she muttered her incantation and the light spell gleamed to life, illuminating all of the loose dust her footsteps had whisked into the air. There did not seem to be any light switches down here, only cold sconces. That was until she found a door decades more modern than everything else down here. The lead to a stairway and at its top was a light switch that activated a long row of lights, illuminating the corridor. She was terribly turned around and could not remember exactly where the costume department was. But after a short while of searching for the door panels, coming across everything from the light box, sound booth, electrical closet, to a few makeshift classrooms, she found it.

With a flick of the switch, the costumes were on bright display, the dusty velvet smell once again filling Jane's lungs. This time, she tried not to be distracted by their elegance.

"Hello?" she asked at first in a whisper, but gaining in strength with every utterance, "Hello?"

"You did remember," a voice sung behind her and she whirled around in surprise. It was a somehow very familiar looking farm boy.

"I...yes. I followed this note."

He was smiling as if he had not had a reason to in quite some time, "You remembered me and you can see me. Thank you."

She nodded, somewhat confused, though she was starting to actually remember being here before, "Why is it that others can't?"

"It's a curse. A Bloodmoon curse."

"Bloodmoon? That's one of the witch covens, isn't it?" he nodded, "You need to tell me about them. I think they hexed my cousin and are coming for me next."

"You must be a Sungaze witch," but Jane could only shrug, "I was around when the feuds began. Long after the trials, the actual witches who survived began to practice their witchcraft away from the city in these woods, the Witching Woods. But they fought over how magic should be practiced. The Sungaze witches said it should be used practically, and to help those who could not be helped through normal means. The Bloodmoon witches said it should be used for power, as a mark of dominance and honor. The feuds ended when the Sungazers managed to strip the Bloodmoons of their power for every day but the blood moon, but on that day they would be exceptionally powerful."

"So they want revenge? To finish what the feuds started?" the boy nodded, "But if they have no power, how did they hex Emma?"

"They have no practical power, not like how you could light a light or blow a wind with a wave of your hand. They can do long, slow spells through gathering items, saying chants, and performing rituals. That can be enough, with the right timing, ingredients, and dedication to create a quite powerful hex."

Jane tried to make sense of it all, "How do you know all of this?"

"I...used to be a Bloodmoon witch, up until they started vying for power. Then I left to return to my family farm. It was fine, I thought I had left it all behind for good but then they started stealing from the town: our herbs, animals, and then, even people. I didn't know what they were planning but it was going to be catastrophic. I went back, tried to sneak in and stop things before they started. But they found me out. I was going to run off, tell all the village who these witches were and what they were doing. But then...they cursed me. They made it so no one could hear or see me but the witches themselves and that even the Sungazers would forget me. Not only that, but they bound me to these woods. Forever. I've been a ghost or the next closest thing ever since then."

"But the feuds were over a century ago. Does that mean..." he nodded, "I'm so sorry."

He looked forlorn, but only briefly, "It's okay. Maybe I wasn't meant to help then. Maybe I was meant to help you now."

"What do you mean?"

"the next blood moon is in about a month so I don't think they're going to hex you. I think they want to lure you out and attack you outright. And you have no chance against a Bloodmoon witch on the night of the blood moon, not without being prepared first. I propose I teach you Bloodmoon magic to defend and prepare yourself for when the time comes. Please, I already failed once. I don't want to stay here wasting away knowing I could have helped."

"Alright. And I'm Jane by the way."

That same sweet smile emerged from a face that had so long been sorrowful, "Ezra."

And from that night forward Jane met Ezra every night in the old theater when the lights had gone out across the campus and the woods were shrouded in darkness. The teaching began with the basics, learning runes of luck and defense, the things she would need most if she was going to survive. Together they crafted talismans and charms which she always wore hidden under her clothes. They were meant to protect her from curses and the dark entropy they wielded. The luck was there to help her get by throwing the odds more in her favor.

However, she certainly wasn't feeling lucky once the sun came up. The witch girls were just as wicked at the name suggested. When the first wash day came around, the girls stayed behind just long enough to make a horrid mess out of Jane's living space with her waste paper basket poured out across her floor, her books and papers sprawled across her desk, and her bed unmade and covered in crumbs. For this and every other mess they made she was tasked with dusting and cleaning the other buildings, the offices of the staff, and even the kitchen. Her reports for the books she had been assigned were torn up, half erased, and soaked in something no matter how many times she rewrote it or where she hid it. Her library books too got battered and ripped and for each one she spent an hour under the librarian's peering eyes sorting and repairing the books. Her uniform was always tampered with so she couldn't wear it properly. Even chunks of her own story book were ripped out so she could not even go to it for comfort.

Yet she had to stay quiet. She had to look sorrowful and powerless in the faces of her tormenters. Ezra said that they could not know she had a plan or had any knowledge of them or the blood moon. He assured her it was the only way to keep their behavior irritating rather than violent.

But because of this, Jane and Ezra began working on a hex. Ezra had seemed a little reluctant as it was that dark power that he associated with those who cursed him. However, once he got started, he seemed fascinated by the possibilities, eager to begin work in the one thing he knew so well. In fact, he seemed more interested in making them suffer for their actions then Jane did. Embarrassment? Scorn? Punishment? What was the best repayment for their heinous deeds? But Jane was much more interested in surviving than taking revenge despite all of the punishment they had inflicted on her.

They decided on a hex of weakness. Many things were required including poppy, willow bark, and the proper parchment. Ezra appeared to know the incantation by heart (or if he didn't he certainly was convincing) and wrote it out in a language Jane did not recognize in a harsh script on the old parchment. He folded the willow and poppy within it and slowly and ceremoniously, they burned it. With the dizzying scent of charred poppy and kindling, the spell took hold and would activate when Jane returned the ashes to the earth. She kept them in a small pouch around her neck until then.

But weakness, they figured, would not be enough. She would need to be offensive as well as defensive if she expected to win. Ezra suggested something a bit different: a spell of earth. With this, the very woods that were the battleground for the feud would fight for Jane and protect her. It was to be powerful, dangerously so, and needed a lot of work. Each day she quietly scavenged for the components, be they from the garden, the gallery, or even the woods themselves. It took nearly two weeks, just barely before the blood moon was set to rise, that they were all gathered. The last item, and the most important, was a drop of her own blood. With this, the components were mixed together in a tiny vial into a phylactery which she also kept discreetly around her neck.

And then the day came, the day preceding the night of the blood moon. Though it was a Sunday, Jane's things were left alone and for once, she was not to spend her weekend afternoon on her hands and knees scrubbing floors. Despite this, she still felt worse than ever with a sour sore festering in the pit of her stomach. She was not sure how or when they would try to lure her away from the campus so she stayed on guard at every moment.

And then there was a knock at the door.

The girls were not in the room, only Lucy who had taken the opportunity to take an afternoon nap. Carefully, slowly, checking her collar for her talisman, ashes, and phylactery, she came to the door. She creaked it open, waiting to be grappled or cursed right then and there.

It was...Penelope, one of Lucy's friends who was always at the stables.

"Hi Jane!" she said chirpily, her riding helmet at her side. There were two other girls behind her, more of her riding friends, "We were wondering since you were free this weekend if you wanted to go riding with us,"

Jane's blinks were slow and heavy and she had to fight back the urge to let out a droning 'uhhh.' Should she? Would it keep her safe? Maybe on horseback, she could just run to safety without fighting, "I, well, I mean..."

"C'mon! You always have to clean on the weekends, why not make up for it and have some fun?"

"Well..." Penelope was looking excitedly expectant, not expecting to hear a no, "okay."

She had only ridden in class on Thursdays, never freely or for fun. But even now fun was hard to come by. Like a scout she was always watching, waiting. Out in the field, she was both exposed and free. But as the day wore on, her suspicion became less and less. She raced, she played, and for once actually enjoyed herself during all the weeks she had spent here.

Then evening came. It was only just the start of sunlight with a bright yellow glow over the horizon. They decided on one more race before the sun went down. It would be down the wooded path, the longest trail the horses had access to. Penelope counted down and the four girls were off. For the beginning, it was a tight match. However, once they hit the difficult terrain of the wooded path, Jane hit her stride. She raced far ahead of the others until she lost sight of them, laughing all the way.

Then she stopped, lost.

The trail had disappeared from her sight and there was nothing but dense trees, "Penelope? Isabel? Karen? Hello?"

And darkness fell quickly, the sun swallowed up by the horizon. And what followed it, of course, was the blood moon.

Then, miraculously, the trotting of horses came from around the corner, the riding girls atop them, "Penelope! Listen, it's dark, we need to go back."

"Oh don't worry, we've been out in the dark lots of times."

"B-but it's going to be lights out soon. We need to go back."

"Are you worried about getting in trouble? It's okay, you don't have to worry about that anymore."

And suddenly she was encapsulated by rope, a net was thrown over her. She was dragged from her horse's back and sank to the tangled ground, meeting the gaze of the Bloodmoon witches. She shrieked. She screamed. Trapped. Fooled.

They dragged her through the woods awhile until they came to a small clearing with an enormous stump in its center, one they laid her across.

Sarah stepped forward, knife in hand, as the other five circled the stump, "So it has come to this, a hundred years of hunting and the final quarry has been captured. From this day forth, it is the blood moon that will reign over the sun, to the one you have gazed at for the last time. I give this honor to you, my lady,"

And from the shadows emerged a tall, wizened figure, face cloaked by the brim of her wide hat. She took up the dagger in her old, bony hand and held it ceremoniously above Jane's helpless body, ready to plunge it into her heart.

It was Headmistress Buckland.

She said something in that old, harsh tongue, and thrust the dagger down. Jane clenched her eyes shut. The sound that followed, the sound of splitting wood.

She had missed and stabbed the trunk and a glowing around Jane's neck told why. But before her luck could be tested again, Jane hurled her wrapped and tangled legs forward, kicking the headmistress in the gut. Jane took hold of the dagger and sliced apart the netting, setting herself free.

"Fool!" Buckland shouted as she got to her feet, "So this will not be so clean, you will still die as ordained. The moon has risen!" and a wash of power poured forth from her hands, throwing Jane off her feet and sending her to the dirt. The girls mimicked, tossing Jane around the woods like a rag doll, cackling she got stamped with bruise after bruise.

"Enough!" a boy's voice scattered in the darkness. Ezra stood in the moonlight dressed in the immaculate sorcerer's garb from the costume closet.

"Oh yes, you," Buckland hissed, "I had forgotten." Ezra's teeth clenched. "Girls, destroy him." She double clapped again and the witches were upon him, hurling him into a towering tree and he fell limp on impact.

"No!"

"Not to worry, Miss Saxon, I haven't forgotten you." All the witches got information and each with a hand lifted her toward the sky, as if in an offering to the moon. The invisible force wrapped around her neck as the witches chanted. With what was left of her energy and control, she ripped the ashen pouch and the phylactery from her neck and threw them to the ground.

They lost their strength as the weakness hit, dropping Jane. But, to her shock, the wooden hand of a gargantuan tree caught her and held her against its trunk. Its brethren swatted the witches, jabbed them with their spiny branches. The grass weaved and tangled, winding around their ankles. The very earth rippled and waved, forcing them all off balance. Then, in a great rumble, a chasm opened in the earth, a dark pit of deep set roots. Each and every witch, despite her struggles, was dragged down into the depths. The earth sealed behind them.

The tree set her down beside Ezra, still laying motionlessly on the ground. Everything then went back to what it was; the earth went still and the trees became trees once more.

"Ezra! Ezra, wake up!" She held his head until his dark eyes gradually opened.

He coughed up a mouthful of dirt and smiled a broken smile, "You did it. A Sungazer and a Bloodmoon. Everything is still balanced....and I am free. Thank you."

Jane smiled back and they embraced each other's bruised and battered bodies in the Witching Woods, waiting until the moon set and the sun rose once again.

SHOUT AT THE DEVIL

JESSICA BARKLEY

Dust swirled in a shaft of light coming through the window. The building was old and faded. Letters on the sign she had passed outside had been bleached by the sun, leaving behind more of a whisper than a declaration: Living Waters Orphanage. Ruth walked quietly down the hall. Finger paintings on yellowed paper clung desperately to the walls. A bulletin board was pinned with pictures of smiling children with sad eyes. Their faces filled her with longing and despair. There were no more laughs here, no more children running down the hall. No more hopeful couples coming to take them home. The orphanage had been closed down for years, sitting here empty with no purpose. Ruth clutched her purse as she continued down the hall. The woman on the phone had said to follow the main entrance to the last door on the right.

Ruth's breath was quick and shallow. Her clothing was black, and her red hair was down around her shoulders. Ever since the incident, she had tried to make herself as inconspicuous as possible. Her long hair was like a wall, protecting her from the rest of the world. It had been hard to talk about it. She was afraid people wouldn't believe her. She needed somewhere to go where people wouldn't judge her or think she was insane. That's when she had seen the ad.

Her favorite coffee shop had a wall set aside for small businesses to advertise. Most of the flyers were for teenagers trying to get jobs mowing lawns or for lost pets in the area. She typically just let her eyes glance over them while she waited in line, not really taking in the words. Something about one of the flyers caught her attention. It had a cross in the middle with text above and below saying, "Survivor support group. Taking back possession of your life after possession." There was a number on the ad to call for more information. Ruth had memorized the number and called later that evening. The woman who answered sounded young and so full of life. She gave Ruth the address and time of the next meeting. Despite desperately wanting help, she still had to force herself to go. The closed down orphanage wasn't exactly a hopeful place to meet.

A sign on the last door on the right had the same flyer Ruth had seen at the coffee shop. Her hands trembled as she reached out for the silver handle on the door. She pushed the door open. The hinges groaned in protest. The room was about the size of a classroom, and there were five chairs arranged in a circle. Four of them were taken. A young blonde woman stood up as she entered, "Hi! You must be Ruth." She extended her hand as Ruth joined them, "I'm Lucy." Her smile looked out of place amidst the dust trailed floor and the grimy windows.

Ruth pried one hand off of her purse strap and shook Lucy's hand, "Nice to meet you." Her voice was timid as she took her seat. The stale air filled her lungs as she breathed in and out. She sat stiffly and looked around at the other members of the group.

"Why don't we go around and introduce ourselves?" Lucy seemed a little too happy for the circumstances. Her bubbly attitude contrasted darkly with the atmosphere of the room. She was like a buzzing neon sign fighting not be swallowed by the night fog. She sat back down and looked at the girl on her left.

"I'm Brandy. It's been two months since my possession." Brandy had dark hair and a small tattoo of a heart on her collarbone. Her sultry eyes peered at them from above her dark, red lips.

"I'm Heather. It's been a year since my possession." Heather was blonde. She wore a tiny gold cross around her neck. Where Lucy's personality was like a buzzing neon sign, Heather's was more delicate, like starlight.

"I'm Jackie. It's been about a month since my possession." Jackie had dark hair with purple streaks in it. Her nails were painted black. She gave Ruth a small, apathetic wave as she spoke. A smirk played across her face.

It was Ruth's turn now. All of their responses had seemed structured. She followed the pattern, "I'm Ruth. It's been two weeks since I was possessed." All of the other girls looked younger than she was. Were they teenagers? Maybe they were in their early twenties? She looked at the wrinkles on her knuckles. She was already in her thirties, and most of her time had been wasted frivolously.

"Good! Everyone is doing great. Who would like to share their story first?" Lucy's eyes sparkled with joy as she looked around the room, "You can tell us how you felt, anything you remember, how you are dealing with it now, and really just anything you feel comfortable sharing." Warmth beamed out of her as she talked.

There was a brief silence. All of the women were waiting to see who would speak first. "I'll go." Heather sat up straighter in her chair, "You would think having a year to process this would make it easier to talk about," she gave a small nervous laugh, "but it doesn't really. I was sixteen when I first became possessed. I don't know why I was chosen, but I think it may have been punishment for my father." Heather made eye contact with the other girls as she spoke. She was more somber now. "My dad performs exorcisms for the church. I think that possessing me was a demonic way to get back at him for years of undoing their work. I grew up around it all the time, but nothing can prepare you for when it happens to you." Heather swallowed before continuing, "I just get bits and pieces when I try to remember." She looked at the floor as if she were searching for answers, "I remember losing pieces of time. Like I would be eating breakfast, and the next time I looked down I was in my room getting ready for bed. Or I would be watching TV, and the next time I blinked I would be cooking dinner. Several times I would be driving, and then I would look up and be in a completely different part of town, as if my body were on autopilot. Everything was disconnected. Nothing is more frightening than not having control over your own body and not remembering how you got somewhere. It was the most terrifying experience I've ever had." She looked up at the group as the other girls nodded. "I still pray every night for protection and for help on overcoming all of this. When I saw your sign," Heather tilted her head towards Lucy, "I just felt like God wanted me to be here for some reason, so that's why I'm here."

"That was an excellent job at sharing!" Lucy smiled reassuringly. "Who would like to go next?"

"I guess I can go." Brandy flipped her hair behind her shoulder. "I was at work when I had my first demonic episode." She paused and cocked her head to the side, "Well at least it's the first one anyone told me about, showed me really."

"What do you mean showed you?" Jackie leaned in as she listened.

"Um, well, they caught it on tape."

"Like, what, a security camera?" Jackie squinted trying to understand.

Lucy straightened her shirt, "Why don't we practice active listening, and just let Brandy talk?" She raised her eyebrow at Jackie who leaned back in her chair and crossed her arms.

"It's ok," Brandy clasped her hands together as she continued. "I used to do adult films. During one of the scenes, I levitated and spouted off some strange language. At first they thought some of the set people were in on the joke, but there weren't any wires. There wasn't really any logical explanation for what happened. Now, no one wants to work with me. No one will hire me. No one who knows anyway. It pretty much ended my career. Honestly, I couldn't believe it was me when I saw the tape. I thought they were playing a joke on me, but the fear in their eyes was real." Brandy took a deep breath, "I called a priest to come talk with me. He said that he believed I was possessed. That's a hard thing to hear, but he helped me through it." Brandy's mouth formed a small smile as she remembered the priest fondly, "I've never really been a religious person, but if there can be something so awful in the world, then there has to be something good, too." Brandy looked up towards the ceiling, "There has to be."

Lucy followed Brandy's gaze then quickly said, "Well done, Brandy. Jackie? Why don't you tell us your story?"

"I didn't want an exorcism. I welcomed my demon." Jackie sat back up as she spoke. Heather leaned away from her as she continued, "He made me feel alive and powerful. All of you were weak. Too weak to truly enjoy it. I bet you didn't even touch yourself during it." She turned towards Brandy, "Did you know that possession leads to heightened sexual pleasure? My climaxes were so intense, it was amazing." Jackie writhed in her chair as she remembered.

"If you honestly enjoyed it," Heather looked disgusted as she talked, "then why did you have an exorcism?"

"It was forced on me." Jackie's face darkened. "My parents talked to the local priests, and they tied me to the bed. Did some holy water, prayers, and stuff. I felt him leave the moment they exorcized him out of me. It was like this gaping hole was left in me, and I was normal again. Disgustingly normal." Jackie leaned back roughly in her chair. The two front legs of her seat came off the ground for a moment from the force before clattering back down. "They're the ones making me come here."

"Well, we are glad you're here, Jackie, no matter the reason." Lucy leaned out and touched Jackie's knee lightly for a moment.

The women turned to look at Ruth, "I guess it's my turn." Ruth's hands were balled into fists, grasping the hem of her shirt. "Honestly, I don't really remember much of the possession." She kept her eyes on the floor, "Everything is hazy. It's hard to sleep at night. I have to leave the lights on. I know it sounds stupid, and that light won't keep me safe, but I don't know what to do. Sometimes," Ruth's voice dropped to a whisper, "I feel like I'm being watched, or I have this unnerving feeling that I shouldn't go to the back of my apartment, and that if I do, something horrible will be waiting for me. It only happens when I'm alone." Tears brimmed up in her eyes, "I don't know. Maybe I'm just paranoid now." She wiped away a tear as it started to fall. "I can't talk to my family or friends about it. They wouldn't believe me. I guess I'm just here hoping to not feel alone at the end of the day. I just need someone to believe me and help me through this." Ruth looked at her feet. Her face was hot with embarrassment as another tear escaped across her cheek.

"Then you have come to the right place." Lucy's voice was soft and kind. "When someone goes through intense emotional or physical trauma, like you all have, sometimes they find themselves feeling like it was their fault. Like they are less worthy of companionship and love because of what they have been through. Like they are broken." Lucy looked at each of the members in turn. "This support group will help you find what you have lost in yourselves." Lucy picked up a bag that was by her feet, "Here, I have one for each of you. I would really like you to write down anything that concerns you, or that you remember about the incident. Sometimes it makes it easier to share if you write it down. I know I have trouble finding the right words sometimes when I'm speaking, but for some reason writing flows easier for me." She passed out a composition book to each of the girls. "On the inside of the cover, I taped one of my business cards. You can call me on my cell any time, day or night. I'm here for you if you need anything, ok?" She smiled kindly as she stood up and folded her metal chair. "I think we had a wonderful first meeting today. Will I see you all again on Wednesday? Same time and place?"

The women nodded and folded their chairs, too. They leaned them against the wall where Lucy had placed her own. Ruth gathered her things and started heading towards the door. She felt a little better knowing she wasn't alone in her experiences, but she was mostly just relieved that it was over for today. As she walked out the door, she heard Lucy ask Jackie to stay behind a moment. The only thing that really made Ruth uncomfortable about the meeting now that it was over was Jackie's story.

Ruth drove home in the fading light and climbed the stairs to her apartment. She plopped her purse on the table and laid the notebook down beside it. All of the lights were still on in her place. She was paying almost double the electric bill that she was before the possession, but for her it was a necessary sacrifice. She couldn't stand the thought of walking into a dark room. Ruth walked to her fridge to find something to eat. It was mostly take out boxes of stale Chinese food and half drank soda cans. She pulled out a box of sweet and sour chicken and grabbed a soda from the door of the fridge. Ruth sat down at her kitchen table and flipped open the cover of her notebook.

Lucy's card was taped to the inside cover with her cell number typed in gold lettering. In the center of the card was a fancy design of swirls underlining her name. The bottom of the card had text from a different language that read, "Natas ot gnoleb uoy." Ruth assumed it was something in Latin as she fumbled through her purse for a pen.

She clicked the pen to get it ready to write. "Dear diary." *This is stupid.* Ruth chastised herself as the ink flowed over the paper. She crossed out the words and started again:

"~~Dear diary.~~ I guess let's just get the hard part over with. My name is Ruth Adams, and I was a victim of demonic possession. I don't know why or how, but I do know that it was real. As much as I would like to think that I imagined everything, I didn't. I don't remember much of the actual possession, but I do remember before and after.

Before all of this started, I was fairly happy. Well, maybe not happy, but at least I was content with my life. I first noticed something weird was going on when small items would disappear from where I left them and then reappear in unlikely places. One time, my phone ended up inside the locked trunk of my car. Another time, my sunglasses that I left at work ended up inside of my dresser drawer. It made me feel like I was losing my mind. There was no way I would have put those items there, but at the time, what other explanation could there have been? I seriously thought that I was having psychotic breaks or blackouts. I even contemplated going to a doctor. That's when the scratches started. Long scratches appeared on the insides of my thighs and across my shoulders. It was like my skin was just splitting apart on its own."

Ruth put down the pen. Even just remembering what happened frightened her. Her heart was beating quickly. Her senses were heightened, and the feeling that she was being watched was back. Ruth glanced towards the back bedroom. That's where her instincts told her something bad was waiting. She turned on the T.V. The sound of other human voices helped to alleviate her anxiety. In a way, it tricked her into not feeling so alone. The uncomfortable feeling still nagged at her. Ruth closed her eyes and prayed, "Dear Lord, heavenly father, please watch over me and protect me from evil. Please keep me safe and protect me from any darkness that may try to come near me." Her lips trembled as she whispered the words. A chill ran across her spine. "Grant me strength to overcome evil, and shield me from demons. In your name I pray, amen." The chill dissipated, and the feeling of being watched was gone. Ruth felt a rush of relief. Exhaustion overwhelmed her suddenly. She sat on the edge of the couch and focused on her breathing, trying to get it back to a normal pace. She curled up on the sofa and pulled a thin blanket over herself. Her eyes closed slowly as infomercials played across the television screen.

Ruth stirred awake the next morning. She showered and dressed quickly. She slung her purse over her shoulder and locked the door behind her. The stair well was grey and smelled faintly of Fabuloso and insecticide. Ruth clambered down the stairs until she reached the first floor. She pushed open the door that led to the lobby. White tiles flecked with grey lined the floor. Ruth made her way out of the apartment building towards her car. The city was starting to wake up. Taxis puttered by with visiting business men in the backseats. A woman jogged along the sidewalk, her ponytail swinging behind her. A young man crossed the street with five, small, yappy dogs leading the way on separate leashes. The smell of cigarette smoke and exhaust drifted through the air. Ruth unlocked the door of her car and climbed in. She drove towards the coffee shop she frequented. In her rearview mirror, she saw a black car hanging back. The vehicle stayed back, but it made the same turns she did. Ruth tightened her grip on the steering wheel. She parked near the front of the coffee shop and bolted inside. She watched through the window as the black car drove by slowly. The windows were tinted, so she couldn't see the driver.

"Hey, Ruth!" The girl behind the counter called out, "Want your usual?"

Ruth tucked her hair behind her ear and turned back towards the counter, "Hey, Jules. Yes, please." She smiled halfheartedly and glanced furtively back out the window.

"You doing ok today?" Jules blended some ice cubes into the coffee mixture.

"Yeah, just didn't sleep well."

"Aww, I'm sorry to hear that. Tell you what, why don't you pick out a pastry? On the house." Jules smiled as she mounded whipped cream on top of Ruth's drink.

"Really?" Ruth's face glowed with gratitude at the unexpected gesture of kindness, "Thank you so much. I really appreciate it."

Jules shrugged, "No problem. You're one of my best customers."

Ruth picked out a flaky pastry drizzled with icing and took her to go bag and her drink from Jules. "Have a good day." She lifted her bag as a substitute to waving since her hands were full.

"You, too!" Jules turned to take the next person's order as Ruth headed back to her car.

More cars were starting to edge their way through the city. Ruth pulled out into traffic to make her monotonous morning drive to the office. Traffic trickled past the buildings and sidewalks. Ruth dug her pastry out of the bag she had stashed in the passenger seat. As she took a bite, some icing fell off and landed on her pants. "Crap." Ruth mumbled through a full mouth as she chewed and tried to brush the crumbs off without leaving any residue. Ruth felt her car bump into something. She looked up to see the black car from earlier in front of her. "Oh no." Ruth whispered as she put her car in park and threw on her emergency flashers.

Ruth stepped out of the car, "I'm so sorry, really. I should have watched where I was going."

A middle aged woman climbed out of the car in front of her. She had blonde hair with a scarf tied around her head. She walked to the back of her car where Ruth's bumper was butted up against hers. "I don't think there's any real damage, do you?" She looked up at Ruth.

"No, it...it looks ok." Ruth looked at the woman pleadingly.

"There's no harm done, child, but why don't we exchange numbers and insurance information just in case?" The woman pulled out a small notepad and a pen and looked at Ruth expectantly.

"Ok." Ruth took the pen and paper and scrawled out her number and the name of her insurance company. She passed the notepad back to the woman.

"Wonderful!" She wrote out her own information and tore out a page. She handed the piece of paper to Ruth. The woman grasped one of Ruth's hands in both of her own as Ruth reached out to take the slip of paper. She leaned in and whispered, "You're in danger."

Ruth stared at her for a moment as the woman crawled back into her car and drove away. She looked at the page she held in her hand. There was a number written on it followed by the words, "I'll be in touch." Ruth slid back into the driver's seat, visibly shaken. Why would a stranger tell her that? Was this some kind of sick joke? Ruth started her car and finished her drive to work.

"You're late, Miss Adams." A tall man was leaned against the edge of the receptionist desk. His bald head reflected the fluorescent lights.

"I know. I'm so sorry, Mr. Thompson." Ruth walked around behind the desk and clocked in on her computer. "It won't happen again."

"Could you bring me a print out of my schedule, please?" Mr. Thompson's voice trailed away as he retreated to his office.

"Yes, Sir." Ruth waited for her computer to warm up so she could pull up the list of meetings for today.

The day dragged by. Ruth's thoughts kept running back to the woman from the accident. She was sure it had been the same car that had followed her to the coffee shop. Why would someone want to follow her? What kind of danger was she in? The questions knotted together in the pit of her stomach.

Ruth made her way to the parking lot after work. She was mindful of her surroundings as she drove home. No sign of the black car. She still had a few hours of daylight left as she eased her beat up Toyota into an empty parking spot close to her apartment building. She trudged up the steps and unlocked her apartment. The lights were out.

Ruth scrambled to find the light switch with her fingers. She flicked the switch and the light came on. Her heart pounded as she eased into the room. Darkness bled from the back of the apartment. Everything looked untouched except for the lights. Ruth went around to the kitchen, bathroom, and living room flipping on all of the light switches. The ominous feeling was being exuded from the back room again. Ruth backed into the lighted area of the living room. Terror coursed through her. She flipped on the T.V. to distract herself. *It's ok.* Ruth tried to calm herself down. *You're ok. Just breathe.* Her heart was still racing, but her breathing was more even now. She walked over to the kitchen table and picked up the pen again.

"After the scratches started forming on my body, I realized that what was happening was like something out of a horror movie. I called a psychic from the want ads to come over, but she wouldn't even come in the apartment. Her face turned pale when I opened the door, and she fled. I didn't want to call my friends or family. They don't believe in spirits. Honestly, at first I thought it was just a ghost. I had done some research online, and poltergeists seemed to be the top result for what I was experiencing.

I booked a hotel room, hoping that it was just attached to something in the apartment, but that didn't help. I woke up in the middle of the night with blood soaking into the sheets and the mattress of the bed. I could feel it sticking to my thighs and my calves. I tried to scream, but it was like all of the air was being driven into my body. I think that's when it really took hold of me.

I don't remember much after that, just flashes of places. I saw my work. I saw my apartment. I saw the outside of the local hospital. Mostly I just remember the smell of rotten eggs when I would come to my senses momentarily. The smell mixed with the intense heat of its presence in a cloud of stifling despair. I couldn't make sense of time or even really the glimpses of things that I saw. It felt like I was drowning constantly in a sea of darkness.

Later, I found out it was the psychic that had told the priests where I lived. She was reason they came to check on me, and honestly, she may be the only reason I'm even still alive at this point."

Ruth put down the pen. The hairs on her arms were standing on end. It felt as though cold fingers had just trailed along the back of her neck. Ruth shivered as goosebumps spread along her body. She shuffled to the fridge and pulled out a bottle of vodka. *Just something to calm my nerves.* Ruth let the chilled liquid burn her throat as she took a swig. The glass bottle clinked against her teeth as she tilted it back down. The alcohol left a trail of fire down her esophagus and into her stomach.

She curled up on the couch as a car dealership commercial flashed its latest deals across the T.V. Ruth tucked her knees closer to her chest and pulled the wrinkled blanket around her. She closed her eyes as the vodka worked its way into her system. Her empty stomach sped up her body's absorption. Her arms and legs started to feel lighter as she drifted off into an intoxicated sleep.

Her dreams were plagued with the screams of babies and figures that darted through the shadows. Ruth could feel fingers entangled in her long hair. Strands of her hair tugged against her scalp. She could feel them rip away from her head. She tried to disentangle herself from where her hair was caught, but the fingers jolted closed and yanked her backwards. The skin on her heels grated against gravel. She struggled to find footing, but the force dragging her was too strong. Suddenly, the ground dropped from beneath her. Ruth plummeted in the darkness; her hair fluttered around her face. Her stomach did flips as she fought to catch her breath.

Ruth's eyes opened as she woke up. She looked around herself. She was on the floor. Her blanket was tangled around her ankles. Her hair was matted with sweat. Early morning television flashed by cheerily in the grey light that seeped through the curtains. She breathed a sigh of relief as she picked herself up off the dusty floor. Cleaning had been put on the back burner lately. She pulled herself to her feet and walked to the shower.

Steam filled the air around her as lavender soap bubbles swirled down the drain. The water helped. It felt clean and safe as she detangled her hair. A clump came out between her fingers. Ruth pulled her hand away, starring at the strands that clung to her palm. She wadded up the ball of hair and stashed it behind the shampoo bottle. Ruth turned off the water and dried herself off. There weren't any visible bald patches. She kneaded her scalp with her finger tips. It was tender to the touch. She got dressed quickly and shoved the notebook in her purse.

Work was monotonous. Clients and schedules and cancelations. The day dragged on until it was finally time to leave the office. Ruth caught herself absentmindedly massaging her scalp throughout the day. It was still sore. She climbed in her car and turned the key. The next meeting would be starting soon. Ruth drove to the orphanage and made her way inside.

Her footsteps echoed down the deserted hall. Ruth opened the door to the room where they met last time. Only Lucy and Jackie were there. The other girls hadn't show up yet. The chairs were already set up. Ruth took the same seat she had last time and placed her purse in her lap. She still wasn't entirely comfortable, especially with Jackie around.

"How are you doing, Ruth?" Lucy looked at her tenderly.

"I had a rough night sleep." Ruth rubbed her scalp.

Lucy clicked her tongue, "Nightmares?"

"Yeah." Ruth looked her a little suspiciously.

"It's normal to experience nightmares when you go through a trauma." A small smile played across her lips, "It's typically just your subconscious trying to make sense of everything that happened to you."

The door opened, and Brandy and Heather walked in. Heather looked over her shoulder, "Did you guys see the blonde in the scarf when you came in?"

"What blonde?" Lucy's voice was a little harsher than she intended.

"Some lady outside." Brandy jerked her thumb towards the front of the building.

"How old did she look?" Ruth was staring at Brandy.

Brandy paused for a moment, "Probably mid to late forties."

"You should all be very careful." Lucy's eyes darted to each of them and her brow furrowed with worry. "We aren't really in the best part of town, and you never know what kind of people are lurking about. You should be especially careful since you are all still very vulnerable."

"What do you mean? Why vulnerable?" Brandy was fiddling nervously with her bracelets.

Lucy looked to Heather who took a deep breath. Heather touched the tiny cross that dangled around her neck, "Your soul is just like any other part of your body. When it gets banged around, it needs time to heal. During an exorcism, the demon who is inhabiting the possessed person clings onto the soul. The priest has to basically rip the demon off of the soul. That—combined with the stress of being inhabited initially—leaves it weak and, well," Heather turned towards Lucy, "vulnerable."

"Exactly." Lucy nodded.

"My dad has actually had multiple patients that have been repossessed after he has performed exorcisms on them. A lot of times they think that he just didn't really get the demon out, but he says it's more like there is a mark on the soul. There's a darkness that draws the evil back to them." Heather sat down softly in her chair.

"So we basically have targets on backs." Brandy scrunched her hair between her fingers as she let out a frustrated sigh and dropped into the empty chair beside Heather.

"On your souls, but yes." Lucy looked at them gravely, "Just please be very careful. Especially if you have all seen this woman lurking about." Her face looked grim and frightened as she looked towards the door, "You never know who might be working against you." Lucy shook her head as if to clear away unwanted thoughts, "Why don't we get back on track?" Her normal smile replaced the tight-lipped frown. "Everyone take your seats. Who would like to share first today?"

"I'll go." It was the first time Jackie had spoken since the meeting began. "I wanted to apologize for the other day. I've been doing a lot of soul searching the past few days, and I think maybe I was just interested in being special. It didn't matter where that came from, as long as I had it." Jackie looked at the floor in embarrassment. "I just wanted to feel like I was a part of something bigger than myself, and having the demon inside me gave me the power to overcome the other things in my life. My home life isn't great. My older brother died when I was thirteen. He was always the golden boy...the one that did everything perfectly." Jackie shuffled her shoes against the floor, "After he died, nothing I could do was good enough. I was living the shadow of a dead person. Everything I did was measured up to his perfect standards. So," Jackie chipped away at her black nail polish, "I decided that if I was never going to be as good as he was, then I was going to be as bad as they played me out to be. I really got into Ouija boards when I was about fourteen. I prayed to Satan every night. I even tried to contact my demonic guardian a few times. It's kind of like a guardian angel, but for the other team." She looked up at the group, "Part of me didn't really believe in it if I'm being honest, but another part always hoped."

"You're a part of this now." Lucy smiled at Jackie warmly, "And we only want you to be you. As cliché as that sounds." She laughed, and it was like tiny bells tinkling. Ruth still felt a little uneasy about Jackie. It seemed like too much of a turnaround for just two days.

"Are we seriously just going to sit here and talk about our feelings instead of doing something?" Brandy ran her fingers through her hair.

"My dad sent me a care package from the Philippines." Heather sat up straighter.

"Good for you, princess." Brandy's agitation bubbled up as she threw a look at Heather.

Heather glared at her, "What I mean is, he's been doing exorcisms over there." She turned back to the rest of the group, "The package had a St. Benedict Crucifix in it and a few bottles of holy water. It also had some Sina Ginger Candy, but I don't think that will help us right now." Heather touched the cross at her throat again as she thought about her dad, "He knows I'm still struggling, and a care package is really the only way he can help me while he's gone."

"That's great." Lucy looked at Heather sympathetically. "Is it in your car?"

"No." Heather shook her head. "It's back at my house."

"Ok, well, why don't you go get it and meet us back here? I think that might make us all feel a little better." Lucy nodded as she spoke.

"Wait!" Ruth called out as Heather began to gather her things. "I don't think you should go alone. It's not safe out there."

"I agree." Lucy's face contorted in concern. "Jackie? Would you go with Heather?"

"Of course." Jackie agreed instantly.

"Oh, no, really," Heather stammered, "I'll be ok."

"Please?" Jackie reached out and touched Heather's arm, "Please, just give me a chance."

Heather paused, looking into Jackie's pleading eyes. She breathed out and nodded her head, "Okay."

Ruth watched as the two of them left the room. She still didn't trust Jackie. Doubt bubbled up in her stomach. "What do we do now?" Ruth's voice came out in a whisper.

"Well," Lucy scooted her chair closer into the circle. The legs scraped along the floor with a drawn-out squeak. "We can still talk."

"I'm gonna go take a piss." Brandy placed her hands on her knees and pushed off.

Lucy waited for the door to click shut behind her as Brandy went to find a bathroom, hopefully one with working plumbing. "It's sad. Some people only want to believe in a higher power when things are looking up." She turned back to Ruth. Her blonde hair framed her face. "Do you want to talk about your nightmares?"

"Not really." Ruth looked at the floor.

"You don't want to know what happened to the babies?"

Ruth's eyes shot up, "What?" Her breath caught in her throat.

"Oh, you know." Lucy stood up and walked behind her chair. She let her fingers trail along the back of it. Her manner was almost seductive. "The ones whose screams you hear at night." Ruth's fingers trembled as Lucy laughed. "Think back to those small little bundles of joy you took so easily from the hospital. Do you remember the way their soft flesh felt against your fingertips? The way their heads needed support?" Lucy mimed holding a baby. "The littlest one grabbed your pinkie. Do you remember his tiny hand? His pink smell?"

Ruth was shaking, "Who are you?"

"No, no, no, let's not rush our time." Lucy clicked her tongue like the ticking of a clock. "I want you to close your eyes and remember."

"I don't—"

"Uh, uh, uh," Lucy wagged her finger, "Eyes closed."

Ruth unwillingly closed her eyes, "I don't remember anything from when—"

"Let me set the scene." Lucy walked soundlessly behind Ruth and crouched so that she could whisper in her ear. "It was a clear night. There was a cool breeze. You were standing on top of a bridge. You could smell the water. The little brats were nestled in the back seat. Then, ever so carefully, you picked them up, one by one, and tossed them over the edge." Lucy's voice escalated in terrifying joy.

"No." A tear slid down Ruth's cheek. Distorted images ran across her eyelids: headlights, a baby blanket, rippling water. "It wasn't me!" Ruth's eyes flared open. "It was whatever was inside of me." Rage and self-hatred flooded through her.

"Ha!" Lucy laughed, "You're too pretty for such copouts. No, it was you. We just helped you do what you always wanted to do." Lucy looked slyly at Ruth, "You were my inspiration for choosing this place, you know. The place that turned you down when you wanted to adopt." Lucy savored every word.

"I *never* wanted to hurt children." Ruth's fingernails dug into her palms.

"No, but you were jealous." Lucy licked her lips, "All those fertility treatments, the sperm donors, because no one could stand your paranoia long enough to get you pregnant the old fashioned way. You're a burden, but you already knew that. That's why you didn't call your family when things started getting really hairy." Lucy pouted, "And even with all the medical marvels they have, you were still barren. Your womb as empty of life as your life was empty of meaning." She spun on her heel with a flourish, "Quite poetic, really. Maybe the universe just knew you would make a terrible mother, and judging by what you did on the top of that bridge, the universe was right."

"Stop it!" Ruth was rocking back and forth as the tears fell freely. She raised her hands to cover her ears, but Lucy only talked louder.

"And you decided that if you couldn't have a baby, then no one would." She punctuated the last four words by shifting her hips from side to side.

"No." Ruth whispered between her sobs. The door shook as if someone was trying to get in.

"Go Away!" Lucy screeched, spinning to face the doorway. Her shoulders hunched up like an animal. She turned back to Ruth, "You are the weakest one. You know that right?" She crossed her arms and leaned down condescendingly. "Look at you. You're pathetic. Crying like a—whoops, I almost said 'baby.'" Lucy cackled.

"If I'm so pathetic," Ruth looked up through tear-matted lashes, "then why even bother?"

"Why, because, darling. You may be pathetic, but you're mine." Lucy ran her finger down Ruth's hair. Ruth pulled away from her.

The door burst open. Lucy growled as she flung her wrist toward the entrance. An empty chair flew towards the door and slammed into Brandy's chest, knocking the wind out of her. Heather stepped over Brandy's limp body followed by the woman in the scarf. Heather had a crucifix in her hand. The woman was evoking angels and praying vehemently. She carried a large, black gun.

"What?" Lucy laughed mockingly, "You think I'm afraid of a gun? I was forged in hellfire, molded with sulfur, and sculpted by time." Her voice deepened as she spoke. The bell-like quality was gone.

The woman kept praying. She aimed the weapon at Lucy. A stream of water surged forth as Lucy's new baritone voice laughed, shaking the window panes with its vibrations. The laughter was cut short as the water hit her face and sizzled against her skin. She squealed in pain and turned away. Ruth could see blisters bubbling to the surface of her cheek and across her left eye.

"Holy water." Heather brandished her crucifix higher. The two women continued approaching steadily.

A growl erupted from Lucy's throat as she twitched her wrist again. Another chair flew from the circle and collided with the scarfed woman's head. A loud smack echoed as she slumped to the floor. Lucy jerked her head to the side. Her neck cracked into a strange angle as she turned her attention to Heather. A toothy grin split across her face.

"Lucifer! In the name of the Father, I expel you! In the name of the Son, I expel you!" Lucy lunged at Heather's throat with her teeth, "In the name of the Holy Spirit, I expel you!" Heather screamed the words with conviction as Lucy's teeth scraped against her skin.

Lucy's body convulsed on the ground. White spit bubbles foamed at the corners of her mouth, and her eyes rolled back into her head. The blisters on her face were swollen with liquid, almost to the point of bursting. Lucy's arms thrashed against the floor. Her head jerked back in one last contraction before a slow exhale wheezed out of her lips. The body went limp.

Ruth walked over to the body slowly, "Is it over?"

"Yes." Heather placed her fingers on Lucy's neck. "No pulse." She looked up at Ruth.

The woman wearing the scarf stirred and sucked air through her teeth. She winced as she sat up and touched her head. Her fingers came away bloody. "She's been dead for a while." The woman stood up and walked over to the girls. "When Satan takes over a body, it's different than when a lesser demon inhabits someone." She wobbled as she tried to maintain her balance. Heather grabbed her elbow to help support her. "Satan takes up more room and burns hotter. The host's soul can't last very long under those conditions."

"Who are you?" Ruth was still trembling as she looked at the woman.

"Well," The woman reached up and straightened her scarf, "I used to be called Sister Mary Eucharist. Now though, I just go by Angela."

"She used to be a nun." Heather helped Angela to one of the chairs that hadn't been flung around the room and then went to check on

Brandy. She talked over her shoulder as she helped Brandy sit up. "She saved me when I got outside with Jackie."

"Where is Jackie?" Ruth looked through the doorway trying to catch a glimpse of her.

"Knocked out on the sidewalk." Angela pulled off her scarf and used it to dab at the blood coming from her head. "She had already been repossessed."

"I think it happened when Lucy asked her to stay late at the last meeting." Heather held up her index finger, and Brandy was following it back and forth with her eyes. "She certainly seemed up for another possession last time." Heather shook her head.

"She'll be ok, but I don't think her body can take another possession." Angela pulled her scarf away and looked at the blood. Her cut was starting to clot. "She's battered, but I don't think that will stop her from opening herself up to evil again." She shook her head.

"Did you know about all this when I hit your car?" Ruth's breath was coming quicker. She was on the verge of a panic attack. Her eyes darted back and forth.

"One of the gifts of the Holy Spirit is discernment." Angela looked at Ruth intently, "And you, child, have such a darkness hanging over you." She tilted her head. I knew something was after you, but I didn't know it was this serious. I followed you. I saw the other girls with the same darkness hovering above them. When I saw the dark haired girl walking out with this one," she gestured to Heather, I took my chance. The demon in her told us about Lucifer's great plan. Demons like to brag, one of their downfalls."

"Do you always carry an exorcism kit with you?" Ruth looked at the water gun leaking on the floor.

Angela smiled, "Honey, when you've seen all the stuff that I've seen, you stay prepared."

Brandy groaned, and Heather helped her up. Ruth lowered her voice, "Do they lie?"

"The demons?" Angela brushed her hair away from her face. "They don't have to lie. They can see into the darkest parts of your soul. That's their way in. The truth is far uglier and more terrifying than any lie could ever be."

Tears streamed down Ruth's face. The images of the babies were seared into her mind now. Vomit seared her throat as she retched on the floor.

Angela stood up and walked over to Ruth. She rubbed her back as Ruth spit up more stomach acid. "Honey, whatever it is you did, God can forgive you if you ask him." Ruth shook her head no and dug her fingernails into her thighs. "Yes, yes, he can." Angela nodded. "Demonic possession brings out the worst in people. You did not have complete control of yourself. Listen to me, they can take even the tiniest seed of evil in your heart and grow it into a terrible force of nature." She stroked Ruth's hair. "What is important now is that you ask forgiveness and live in the light. Just make the most of what time you have left here." Ruth turned and rested her forehead on Angela's shoulder. "Would you like me to pray for you?" Angela's voice was soft and comforting as Ruth nodded. "Our Father, who art in heaven, hallowed be thy name. We humbly come before you to thank you for this victory today and ask for your help once again." Ruth felt Heather place her hand on her shoulder as Angela prayed. "Please bless this broken child and help mend the wounds, both spiritual and physical that have been left behind by this attack. Surround her with your love and grace, and give her the strength to make it through this trial in her life. Lord, we know you only give us what we can handle, and judging by the amount of tribulation you have placed on this girl, you must think she is so strong." Ruth felt Brandy's hand rest on her other shoulder. "Help us to stay on your path, and may your will be done on Earth as it is in heaven." Brandy and Heather joined Angela in unison, "Amen."

"Amen." Ruth whispered. Some of the weight lifted off of her chest as she pulled away and looked at the three of them. "Thank you."

The days to come were marked by depression for Ruth. She struggled with the torment of what she had done. The nightmares persisted. She, Brandy, and Heather attended survivor meetings led by Angela every Saturday. Brandy eventually got a job as a photographer. She found that spending her life behind the camera gave her more joy than her time in front of it. Some of her clients recognized her from her porn career, but mostly that just helped to put them more at ease with her. The old adage of 'imagine your audience naked' was just a little easier for them. Heather's father came back from the Philippines, and she joined him in performing exorcisms. She often joked that after exorcising Satan, lesser demons were a piece of cake. She helped to calm the patients, but in the meetings she confessed she was still terrified during every session. Angela mentored the girls and did her best to help them with their own struggles. Jackie died a few weeks after they performed her second exorcism. They found a business card beside her body with the text 'Natas ot gnoleb uoy' typed in gold. Under the text, Jackie had sloppily scribbled the words backwards and in reverse order: you belong to Satan. Her eyes could not be closed, and her cracked lips were peeled back in a toothy grin. Her family chose not to have an open casket.

THE SCARRED

TINA FORTH

She wasn't always called Narla. In her past, she was known by another name and lived in a forest made of stone on an island off the coast of a vast land. Narla couldn't remember much about those days. They seemed hazy in her mind, because many winters had passed by her since she lived in the stone city. She thought of herself as Narla and it was all that mattered.

Narla liked to sit in her favorite tree in the forest and watch the vultures soar high in the sky. Those beautiful birds spent the entire afternoon in the up there and barely flapped a wing. She remembered the time one of them tried to land on a cliff and missed it four times. Each time the magnificent bird would return for another pass until it finally found a place to land. The vultures were her friends. She knew they watched out for her and let her know when there was danger in the forest. If she followed them, they would show her things to eat.

She'd lived in the forest ever since the night she was taken to it by the tribe. The tribe consisted of very bad people who did horrible things to women. Narla remembered when she lived in the stone city and knew people like her. Those days were long gone, but she was happy. So long as she could find food and a safe place to sleep, she was very happy. There were bears and wolves in the forest, but she'd learned to avoid them. Bears could be sent running if you hit them in the nose with a stone.

That day, Narla sat on the branch of her favorite tree and watched the birds on the end of her limb. She was hungry and the birds had a nest of eggs. Those eggs would keep her fed for another day. Narla didn't mind if she spent the entire morning near the nest. All she needed to do was sit in place and the birds would forget she was there. The birds might smell her, but Narla took care to roll in some pinesap before she climbed the trees that day. The forest was mostly pine in this part and the birds wouldn't notice her smell. She sat there on the branch and held a place with her feet. Her hands grabbed the branch on which she perched. Every hour she advanced another foot toward the nest. The birds didn't notice even when the branch slipped down each time she moved toward them.

Sometimes Narla would remember the tribe and what they did to her. How she was grabbed from the stone city and taken to the forest. So much was blank in her mind. All she needed to know, she remembered. But every so often, she would remember the tribe and what it had done to her. How each of them did horrible things and dumped her in the forest. The worst was when the man hit her in the head with a rock. Narla almost died the first week as she wondered around senseless. Then she found some wild onions and they tasted good.

"I swear to God," Robert said to Bo as they walked down the trail, "that crazy lady is somewhere out here. I know because I've seen her in the past." He turned and peered at a shadow in the tree line, but it was just a limb.

"That's what you said about the ghost of Matilda Gray," Bo snapped back at him. "Didn't you say she came one night and threatened to kill you? Didn't you tell us this is why you married her daughter?"

"Different situation," Robert replied. "It was the only way her daughter would ever consent to marry me. So I played on her superstitions." Every man in the hunting party had a laugh.

There were five of them in Northwestern Pennsylvania that afternoon. Hunting season had begun and they could take time off from their work to look for deer. All of them carried shotguns, although Howard brought along a rifle from the European War. They'd been up late that night distilling off the last of the hooch for the buyer who was supposed to pick it up from them in a week for his speakeasy. Business was good and there were plenty of people who wanted it, even if congress had banned the sale of alcoholic beverages in the United States. So long as Wall Street made everyone rich, there was no reason to keep out of the party.

Bo was out in the front. At twenty-eight, he was the leader of the band and knew how to make the hooch. Buck was his brother and two years younger. Robert knew about the process of fermenting a batch of corn and found them a campsite in the woods to use. David was a cousin who was twenty and wanted in on the operation. The last member of their party was Howard, who was from another branch of the family in Maine. They had a nice little operation hidden away in the woods on the other side of the mountain and didn't worry about anyone interfering with it.

They didn't know that Howard was with the federal government.

The revenue men had tracked the illegal booze operation, which supplied so much jackleg whiskey to Pittsburgh months ago. It was a serious matter to have one of their people on the inside. This was not easy to do since most of these local families went back generations and didn't talk much to outsiders. Howard was one of Mr. Hoover's new men who rose up through the ranks and had a spotless record. When the chance came to infiltrate a bootlegging operation in Pennsylvania, he jumped at the opportunity.

"So how do you know so much about this crazy lady?" Howard asked Robert. "It sounds like you're some kind of expert." He played the role of an out-of-state relative who needed work and wasn't too bright.

"Because I was one of the men Sheriff Sanders deputized to find her," he told his friends. "Back when that lady from the city disappeared around here. You know, the lady whose purse they found near the reservoir."

Howard nodded as if he knew a little bit, but not much. In fact, Howard the government agent worked on that case. The local county contacted Washington for help as she was from a family of quality and it made them all look bad at the courthouse. Poor little rich girl goes missing from the streets of Pittsburgh. Her car is found in a forest near the North West Pennsylvania federal land (another reason to call Washington). Government men swoop all over the woods, but they don't find a thing. Another mysterious disappearance for the history books.

Howard knew more about the case than he wanted to admit. It broke his heart when he found out what happened and who did it. He didn't like to think much about it. Many years had gone by since it happened.

Narla was about to move forward on her branch when she saw the tribe move below her. What was this? The tribe never ventured into her forest, they knew what would happen. This was her land and she protected everything in it. She stood still and became a part of the tree as the tribesmen moved under her on the old trail. There were only a few of them. It caused her to remember the night she was taken to the forest. It was men like the ones below Narla who did those things to her.

She stopped her observation of them and tried to remember what happened. Something about trusting them and why she'd let them take her to this place. She felt funny in the head and crept back to the tree. The birds noticed her, but she wasn't very hungry all of the sudden. Narla held onto the tree trunk and became part of it as she watched the tribe slide past her position and vanish into the forest.

This was her forest and she would defend it. The naked young woman slipped down from the tree and hid behind a bush. She didn't resemble anything civilized, with her long tattered hair and mud-covered skin. Narla didn't appear to be anything human. She dropped to the ground, whistling like a bird just in case anyone looked in her direction, and began to circle around the tribesmen. She could follow them until the time was right to act.

The sharp knife was still under the rock where she left it. Narla found it last year foraging through the old cabin. It held a good edge and she used it as a tool. Lashed to a stick, it was excellent for catching fish. She took it out of its hiding place and moved back to where she saw the tribe on the move. Soon they would leave unless they planned to stay here. She still hadn't decided what to do about them.

Then Narla saw the man with the stick in the back of the column. She remembered that stick. Narla recalled a man who held it to her head while the others did things to her. Her thoughts were garbled and she couldn't remember much about what happened afterward, but the stick she did remember. It made loud sounds and she was scarred of it.

If he held the stick, it must be the same man who caused her so much pain. Then she noticed all the tribesmen carried sticks. These had to be the same men who dumped her in these woods years ago. Narla ran her finger along the sharp blade of her knife. There was a sickness in the forest and she needed to cut it out.

"Is this the place you talked about?" Bo said to Robert. "The way you talked, I thought it was some kind of palace.

"Just an old cabin," Robert replied. He was the biggest man out of the party but didn't eat all that much.

David propped his shotgun against the tree outside and looked at the old cabin. It still had a roof, but the entrance didn't have a door on it. There was a small porch, but he did trust the eaves over it. Howard, his rifle cradled under his arm, walked into the cabin and looked around. Not much left, hard to say who built it or why.

Howard tried to look his most innocent. They'd accepted him as one of the family all week and he'd done his best to earn their trust as he helped them distill the hooch. Several barrels were already in the back of the truck at the other camp. No one would bother it while they were out here. No one was supposed to know about the other camp. All he needed to do was contact someone in Washington when they left the camp and it would be cleaned-up. He didn't like betraying these men, but there were laws. Plus, he wanted that promotion.

They decided to make camp in front of the cabin as no one wanted to sleep inside it. The men unpacked their bedrolls and put up some canvas overhead just in case it rained. It was going to be a good weekend of hunting before they had to get back to the stock. Howard joined them around the fire and made up a few tales of fishing in Maine to keep them interested. However, for the most part, he allowed them to talk while he remained silent. They gave him useful evidence he could use later.

They found David's body in the morning. Bo got up first that morning to get the fire started and went out to take a piss after it was going. He'd dropped his pants when he noticed a boot that stuck out from behind a tree. After he buttoned his pants, Bo crunched through the old undergrowth to see who it was. They'd all had a bit too much of the stock last night and assumed it was one of the crew.

"So which one of you...." he started to say before he looked down and saw David slumped up against the tree with his throat cut out. His blood was dry, as it had drained hours ago.

The best they could figure was that it happened sometime in the night. Howard didn't want to give his cover away, but he could tell it was done with a knife. A big one, given the slash marks. It was quick and David never had the chance to scream.

"The crazy lady," Bo said as they stared down at the body.

It didn't take Narla long to take care of the first member of the tribe. He was foolish. All she needed to do was sit and wait for someone to venture outside of their camp that night. She stood perfectly still all evening in her most stone pose. Narla perfected the pose the first year she lived in the forest. For a week after she came to the forest, Narla sat in one spot and did not move. She drank the water from the rain and managed to chew on some food she had with her. Her weight dropped quickly, but she didn't care. Inside her mind, she was dead and waited to fade into nothingness. Eventually, she did become nothing. After the week of sitting in the same place, she began to move. Just a little bit. Then she moved enough to crawl across the ground and find something to eat. It wasn't hard; she seemed to know what plants were good for her and which ones would bring instant death.

Narla became something between animal and human that crept on the ground to survive and hid in the dark. She located a cave to stay inside when the weather was bad and soon taught her how to crawl up a tree when a bear threatened her. She had no sense of who she was or what she'd been. All such information was gone, stolen from her when the men took her into the woods. The rock to the head was the final thing that caused her to lose her sense of self. They'd left her for dead, but she became something else. None of the men thought she was still alive or they'd have taken care of her earlier.

As she grew stronger, Narla learned to steal food and clothes from the farms near the forest. Stories spread of a wild woman who lived in the forest and hunters were told to watch out for her. Other people confused her with a woman who lost her mind and ran off into the forest, never to be seen again. Narla had a keen sense of danger by now and would vanish up a tree or into a grove if she heard anything, which suggested the tribe to her. Other people were always the tribe to her, as she had no other concept of them.

But this group was different. There was something about them that brought back the memories of what sent her to the forest. She knew they would contaminate the forest and kill the only place she knew as home. Narla wasn't about to allow that to happen. As she watched, the others gather around the dead body on the ground, she ran her thumb along the knife blade again and waited. They might try to leave, but they still had her to consider.

"His throat cut ear-to-ear," Bo said the rest of the group. "Who would do this? Your crazy lady wouldn't know how. This has to be the work of those boys from Slippery Rock."

There was another gang of bootleggers from Slippery Rock who wanted to muscle in on their hooch operation. Howard knew about them from his office in New York City. Many of these small-timer operations were consolidating in the wake of increased pressure from the federals. It made sense as a way to save and hide materials when the government constantly tried to locate them. Howard adjusted his jacket and scanned the area with concentration. Somehow, he didn't think it was the rival gang, but he couldn't let them know his reasons.

"I don't think it's the Slippery Rock gang," Robert said as he looked at the body. "They wouldn't have used a knife. That bunch would have taken us all out at once. They brought back those Thompsons from the war and like to use them."

"We need to get out of here," Buck said to the rest of the band. "There could be more of them in the woods just waiting to kill us all. And what about the stock we left at our camp? If these are the Slippery Rock Boys, they'll go right for it. We'd be left with our pants down and nothing to deliver to the buyers." He picked up his shotgun and loaded two shells into it.

"Yeah," Bo agreed. "We need to get moving." He gave orders, just like in the war, to the other men to break camp and head back to the base.

"No reason to stay here another night," he told them. "And keep a watch for any strange movement out there. Some of these old boys know the woods just as good as we do."

Howard kept his eyes on the terrain at all times while he rolled up his blanket. He didn't think it was the rival gang. Just not their style. Someone wanted to send them a message. Perhaps it was the crazy lady they talked about, but crazy people seldom had the mental reasoning to carry out a murder such as this. It appeared to be the style of someone who wanted to see them all gone or dead. Howard worried the second option was what they had in mind.

"Has anyone seen Buck?" Bo asked them, as they made ready to leave. The group packed everything quick and was ready to go in an hour. Buck wanted to take the body with them, but Bo overruled him and said it was a matter for the sheriff, who was in their pocket. He'd let the sheriff know where the body could be found after they delivered the hooch. They would give David's share to his family. Let the law deal with whoever killed him. They would have to move their operations and the law could make things bad for Slippery Rock. Besides, everyone just wanted to get out of there.

Narla watched them break camp and prepare to leave. The memories of what happened to her continued to flood her mind and she had a hard time to remain still on the tree branch where she watched them. Yesterday's kill was easy. He didn't even see her until she came up behind him and touched his shoulder. It was so much easier than a deer or bear as the tribesman didn't even have fur over most of his body. One slash and he went down. She was careful to aim her cut right below his face to do the most damage.

When he went down, Narla wondered what to do about him. The body wasn't of much use to her and she didn't want to cause the others to scatter until the sun came up. She finally decided the man was best displayed in a way that would scare the others away from the forest. Narla spent an hour or so arranging the body in the best way possible. She even placed flowers all over him to let the others know it wasn't a bear. Bears didn't hurt people too often, but they had no way to know it.

From her spot on the limb, she waited until one of the tribesmen would move in her range. She watched one of them argue with a man who appeared to be in charge. The rest packed and wanted to leave in a hurry. This wasn't what Narla wanted. She wanted them to be scared and terrified of her. She wanted these men to know who was responsible and let the others know it would happen to them if they ever moved into the forest where she lived. She only needed one of them to survive and tell the others.

Narla hopped down the tree limbs. She noticed one man had left the larger party and went back the body for some reason. He seemed to be angry. She didn't want two of them in the same place and it would be hard to carry off any one of them. It was better the bodies be spaced out for maximum effect. This wasn't too much of a problem since they were all ready to move and this would make it easy for her.

Buck was headed back to the location of David's body when he heard something hit the dirt behind him. He spun around with the shotgun, terrified it was one of the gang come back to finish the rest of them off. He didn't see a thing behind him. Dammit, what kind of family would they be to leave David's body back there to be chewed up by the animals? One of his uncles died in the woods years ago and they still talked about how disgusting he looked when he was found.

Relieved there was nothing behind him, Buck adjusted his wool cap and turned back to the trail. He planned to haul David's body back himself and tell the sheriff it was an accident. They could take care of the matter in the family and not have to involve outsiders. What kind of family was it where you had to bring in the law for what they needed to handle on your own? The law would make things worse for them. He began to hum and continued to the tree where David's body was left.

Buck stopped. There was a pile of leaves in front of him. It blocked the trail. This wasn't right; there had been anything in the middle of the trail when they went to examine David's body the first time. He stopped and looked at the pile. It wasn't very big and hugged the ground. Could some animal have swept it out here? Was it the wind? He went over and gave the pile a gentle kick, expecting it to move off the trail.

The pile of leaves grabbed his ankle and pulled him to the ground.

Out of the leaf pile, a figure emerged with mud for a body and matted hair for a head. Buck was terrified by the vision in front of him and froze. When it moved in his direction, he tried to find his shotgun, but it was too late. Narla was on top of him in seconds.

Buck tried to push the demon off him, but she held onto his arm and had the advantage of surprise. Narla brought her knife down in an arch and stabbed Buck through the eye and into his brain. The last thing she saw was a tiny woman coated with dirt who plunged a knife into him. Buck gagged and was silent.

Narla looked down at him as she wiped off her blade on his shirt. Next, she looked up and wondered how long it would take his friends to notice he was gone. Probably not, long. This would be the first place they'd look once someone noticed he wasn't with the rest of the group.

She wanted to prepare him as she'd don't the other, but the flowers were out of the question. Narla drug him across the trail and positioned him on one of the many trees. She took out her knife and carved a pretty shape several times over him. This would let the rest of them know who did it. Hadn't they told her how much she was loved when they got her into the car? She placed one hand on her head and tried to remember some more thoughts, but they were all so hard to recall.

Robert was the one who took off first to find Buck. Bo watched him leave and then decided they all should accompany him. It was obvious Buck went back to get David's body since he was no fan of leaving him.

"I need to explain a few things to him," he grumbled with the others who trailed behind. "I'm in charge here and he is going to do as I...."

And then they found the body of Buck.

"A knife again," Bo, said to the rest of the men as they glanced nervously at the trees. "Maybe you all will listen to me in the future. We have to get out of here now and don't ask me about what to do with this body." The men began to back out of the trail and headed in the direction of the broken campsite.

Howard looked the body over carefully before he left. Who would care Valentine's hearts into the body of a victim?

Narla was very still again as the tribesmen came upon the body of the man she'd killed. She didn't know if the leaf pile trick would work with him. It had with the bears and rabbits, but she didn't know how much the tribesmen used smell to track their pray. She'd seen them move around in the past and didn't understand how they found game. She used her eyes and sense of observation. The larger animals relied on smell a lot, but she could always out think them if she had to do it.

Narla watched them move away quicker this time. It didn't surprise her; they wanted to get away from her, even if they didn't know where she was at the time. The only thing Narla had going for her was her stealth. She was half the size of most of those men and couldn't engage them in a direct fight. However, like with the bears, she didn't have to fight them if she wanted to kill one.

She let them get far enough down the trail before she left her perch on the tree limb. Narla could smell the fear from them, which was good for her. She decided to wait before she struck again. It would take them a few hours to get out of her forest. In a few hours, they would become complacent again and she could strike once more. She had to be careful of those sticks they carried that made such a loud noise. She's seen what they could do in the past and didn't want to be on the receiving end of it.

This time she followed them on the ground. The forest was quiet, but there were always plenty of animals in the background. She watched them use their sticks at a fox, but it was too fast for them. One of the tribesmen grabbed a man who'd used his stick too quick and an argument ensued.

Hours later, one of the tribesmen fell back. He was a little bit tired and couldn't keep up with the rest. Narla crept closer and closer each time, careful to avoid the sticks on the ground that might snap. All the years she'd lived in the forest taught her to watch out for anything that could make any noise. Several times, she nearly starved after losing a rabbit when it heard her in the background. She crawled after the tribe on the ground and smelled the rich sent of soil as she went along. It was an odor that always managed to comfort her.

Howard was scared.

In all the years he'd worked as a government agent he'd never felt such terror. He was ready to tell the others who he really was, but they would kill him on the spot. Even if he took them out first, he'd still have to contend with whoever had killed the two men. Someone or something wanted them all dead. This couldn't be the work of a rival bootlegger gang. If it were the Slippery Rock gang, his party would all be dead by now from bullets. The other two men were dead from a knife wound. A knife wound. Who used knives with such skill these days? A knife was the tool of a low-class thug, not a professional assassin. Whoever killed those men was a professional in every aspect.

It was down to Bo, Robert, and Howard. Bo still led the group and Howard didn't see any reason to argue. If they were attacked in the open, he might try to do things his way, but for now, it made sense to stay together and try to survive. Robert kept muttering under his breath about the crazy lady and Howard wanted to tell him to shut up.

"It's her, I tell you," Robert kept saying. "She's been out here for years. Ever since we found that purse from the city. I know she came with those men and they left her." Robert had the gun loaded and constantly spun it in every direction.

Howard, who was right in front of him stopped. "What did you just say about the purse and 'those men'? He looked Robert directly in the face.

"The ones I saw her with when they drove up here," Robert gasped. He didn't seem to be concentrating on what he said.

"Robert, shut up!" Bo snapped in front of them both. "He doesn't need to hear any of your ghost stories. I'm worried about the human kind after us!" Bo dropped his shotgun and aimed at some movement, but lifted it when she realized the source was a squirrel.

"No, I want to hear what you were trying to tell me," Howard grabbed him by the shoulder. He prayed they were too concerned about survival to wonder why he wanted to know.

"I saw five men and a woman drive up here in a car about ten years ago," Robert told him, his eyes constantly on the trees. "They looked like they were having some party, but she looked scared. Right after that was when we started hearing about the crazy lady. I think she had something to do with them." Robert pulled away and walked behind Bo.

Howard kept his rifle ready, but he hoped it was a human killer he needed to worry about. What Robert told him was too similar to something from his past from ten years ago. Right after the doughboys came home from France. He closed his eyes and tried not to think about Nancy, she would never come back. They never did find a body, but he'd used his connections to make sure the men responsible never would hurt anyone again.

The sky was darkened by the section of the forest. This was a section of old growth where the trees grew together and blotted out the sunshine. Although it wasn't even noon by his pocket watch, Howard was worried they wouldn't make it out by dark to the camp where the bootleggers distilled the alcohol. He was worried about Robert and the way he continued to spin around with his shotgun, ready to shoot at anything. Like the rest of the crew, he was a mountain boy raised on the stories of Nittany lions, although they no longer roamed the hills.

A mountain lion wouldn't use a knife, Howard knew. Bo still walked out in front of both of them as if he was on picket duty back in France. This was a different sort of danger. No gas shells fell from the sky, but they still had to worry about what might kill them.

She almost had him.

Howard fell back from the other two men on the trail. He was tired and wanted to get out of the forest, but they still had miles to walk. There was plenty of mud underfoot, the rain was heavy this fall and he'd spent plenty of time in it. Howard heard a sound of leaves behind him and turned around, expecting to see a squirrel again.

It was a woman. She wasn't that tall. The woman was naked, save for the mud all over her and the leaves that stuck in them. She stood there and looked at Howard for a few seconds before her knife came out. Howard brought up his rifle and she froze. The woman knew what it could do. She stood there in all her glory and resembled something out of a fairy tale.

And then a light of recognition came in her eye. She looked at him and seemed to remember something. Her knife went down and she changed personality before his eyes.

"How-ard," she forced herself to say.

Narla seemed to remember something about this man now that she could see him up close. Her mind couldn't recall much because of the stone that one of her rapists tried to kill her with that day. She tried hard to remember this man and what he once meant to her. There was too much damage in her head to allow Narla to put it all together. Nancy Adkins turned into Narla of the forest on that day six years ago and there was no going back.

She wanted to remember. She wanted to remember badly. Howard watched as a single tear flow down her face.

The shotgun blast from Bo ended her problems. Howard stood there and watched Nancy go down to the ground.

"I got her," Bo announced. "At least we know who was trying to kill us."

"And who killed David and Buck," Robert agreed. They rushed over to the body.

She died still with the knife in her hand. The three men looked her over and tried to figure out where she'd come from. It wasn't easy to tell under the mud. Finally, Howard pushed the other two aside and scrapped some of the dirt away so they could get a good look at her. The face seemed familiar.

"Lookitthat!" Robert yelled. "She's got a ring on her finger!"

Howard knelt over and slipped it off her hand. It was loose because she still weighed a lot less than she did years ago after living in the forest. The mark on her head was consistent from what the man had confessed to him. The ring he'd given her before she was abducted confirmed it.

"Damn," Bo sighed, "That was one crazy bitch. You have to split the ring with us, Howie. We're all in this together."

"I guess we are," Howard agreed. "Good shot, by the way. I learned to shoot too while I was in the army. Is that where you learned?"

"Hell," Robert said. "We've all been shooting since we were kids. Let's get out of here, no reason to stick around, we plugged the crazy lady and that's all the law will want to know."

"True," Howard told him. "You guys want to know something?" Howard cradled his rifle as he backed up in the woods.

"What?" Bo laughed. "You got something special to tell us? After today I don't need to learn anything new."

"You need to learn this," Howard explained. "I'm with the federal government. You're both under arrest."

The bootleggers went for their guns, but Howard was faster.

As he ripped holes in the drums of hooch and let them drain on the ground, Howard thought about what his official story would be. He'd buried her deep in the woods and she wasn't supposed to still be alive anyway. The other bootleggers might be a problem, but he could always claim a fight broke out over the way the money was split.

He'd done his job and that was all his employers would care about.

Some jobs needed to be finished on your own.

THE SCREAMS OF GHOSTS

ALEXIS RAYE

As she was about to close her email for the night and go to sleep, Sara heard that familiar little beep. A new message was waiting for her. It was an email sent through her YouTube account, which she had filtered as soon as her channel had taken off. It was only 9 months ago that she started uploading videos of her adventures but she had really started ghost hunting years earlier. As a kid, she and her brother would dare each other to go into the creepy abandoned houses on the other side of town. They fascinated her with their old architecture and their decrepit walls. She couldn't believe that houses that looked so lifeless, used to be alive with the sounds of families. Somehow, they never scared her, though she pretended to be for her brother.

She truly loved exploring them. What she loved even more was the attention she got from telling her friends about her brave trips inside. She never had enough of that. From the age of 8 and all the way through high school, she regaled anyone who would listen of dark stories filled with supernatural events that she made up off the cuff. Not everyone believed her but it was hard to deny how good of a story teller she was.

And as a new college graduate from a media arts school, she had dedicated her first year of adulthood into creating this persona of an extreme ghost hunter. Her success was overwhelming, even to her, and her fame seemed to grow exponentially every day. She was now even recognized on the street and asked for autographs. That, of course, made all of her sleepless nights and uncomfortable overnight stays in creepy old houses worth it.

The email was still bold as she clicked on it. It was an invitation to fly across the country to Louisiana sent from "The Conservation Collective of Pre-Civil War Phantasmal Plantations". She read it carefully.

Dear Ms. Sara Elliot,

The Conservation Collective of Pre-Civil War Phantasmal Plantations would like to extend an invitation for you and your crew to spend a night in one of our oldest and most spectral houses. It is called "The Lynch Plantation" named after its original owner, although its name holds appropriately with its history. Mr. Lynch was said to be the cruelest man in the south and lynched all of his slaves when he found out that the war had been won by the north. Surprisingly though, his story is not the one that the locals remember. Called Pi Beta Die by the locals, this house's last use was to house a sorority for the local university. 15 years ago, the maintenance man assigned to the house had a psychotic break and killed all 24 members of the sorority then hung himself on the porch outside.

It is our belief that the Lynch Plantation's history is enough to interest you but to further encourage you to create an episode for this house, we have arranged all of your travel and accommodations. You will see the details in the attached document.

The Conservation Collective of Pre-Civil War Phantasmal Plantations seeks to get more publicity and therefore more funding for our cause so please send your reply as soon as possible.

Best Wishes,

The CCPCWPP

She was hooked. Instead of going to bed as planned, she stayed up all night reading and researching the sordid history of the plantation. It was even more incredible, terrifying and mysterious than they had let on in the email. She knew that a night in this house would solidify her as YouTube's leading Ghost Hunter and may even lead to her getting her own show. She knew her fans well. They would love the creepy historical aspect and eat up the sorority massacre with a spoon. When she was too excited to wait, she dialed the number of her main camera tech Lila.

"Its 6:45am Sara, you better have actually seen a ghost," she grumbled. Lila wasn't a morning person and she had known Sara for long enough to know that most of her "ghost sightings" were fake and in fact was one of the people responsible for how real their "encounters" looked.

"Lila, if you wake up now and listen, I'll buy you Starbucks and give you a raise," Sara said. She knew Lila couldn't resist coffee.

"What is it?" she asked, sighing.

Sara beamed with enthusiasm. She knew that it was coming across through the phone because as she explained the email, Lila became more and more alert and excited.

"This could be huge for us Sara!"

"So you're in?" Sara said, knowing that she didn't even need to ask.

"Duh!"

"Ok ,we have to get the guys to agree too." Sara coached.

"Just promise them an adventure and to keep them when you get your own show," Lila said nonchalantly. Of course the rest of the crew would agree. The guys were in their mid-twenties and could be pacified with a cheeseburger.

The next few days were filled with preparation. Sara responded to the email to agree to the trip and outlined what she needed when they arrive and explained who she was bringing. The impression she got from the responses were that the more the merrier. Finally, they were all on a plane from Washington to Louisiana. The guys slept the whole way, snoring loudly of course. Sara and Lila sat together to write the script for the background and opening. They would shoot the outside of the plantation and house during the day and have shots of Sara explaining all the details she found about the mass lynching and murders.

By time they arrived, Sara and Lila had all of their shots planned and a script all laid out. Even though they were itching to go straight to the old house, The Conservation Collective of Pre-Civil War Phantasmal Plantations contact insisted they check into a hotel and get settled and rested. They would begin their investigation and shooting tomorrow. They were all smiles and splurged on room service and watched TV on the flat screen. The hotel was obviously very old but well-kept and the rooms were modernized for the guests' comfort. The lobby was small but elegant with two rows of white pillars that led out to the street. After they were stuffed, they decided they needed to walk it off by exploring the bustling town around them.

It was a warm October night so they skipped their jackets and made their way down the old fashioned road. The buildings were tall and thin and the antique street lights cast long shadows against them which no one else seemed to notice. The group weaved their way in and out of the busy streets watching the locals as they enjoyed the many bars and cafes. Andrew, one of the sound techs was mesmerized by the voodoo shops he saw and dragged Colin, another camera guy, in with him. He bought them all incense and they laughed as they all wandered the streets with the potent twigs. Finally they settled on a quiet smoky café. Knowing they had to be awake and alert the next day, they all opted for coffee or tea. As they sipped the delicious, hot beverages, they began to discuss the plan for the next day.

"Ok, I think we should be all packed by 11am. I want to make sure we can get to the location and have plenty of time to explore the plantation before sunset. We also need time to shoot the outside shots with the narrative and set up camp inside for the night," Sara said.

"I agree," Lila said. "Colin, I know you have that 4k camera that can work in low light. Hoorah for that. I was thinking we'll start outside and work our way in. We'll shoot like we always do, start in the living room, I'll explain the history of the house then we'll pretend we'll hear something and head upstairs."

"You want me to add a sound effect in post?" Colin asked.

"Yeah, of course," Lila said. "As long as its not too cheesy. Has to sound real. Like a ghost screaming or something."

"I have no idea what that would sound like," Colin laughed.

Lila covered her mouth and made a groaning sound. "Like that."

"Sounds like a bullfrog with indigestion."

Well, you know what I mean. We'll worry about all that later."

"Done deal."

"Of course, we will have to wait until we see it in person to make the final decisions but Sara and I have pretty much memorized the property maps and house floorplans." Lila finished.

"How creepy is it that it's called "Lynch"?" Andrew said.

Matt, their back-end video editor, chewed on some cookies as Andrew glanced his way.

"What? Just cuz I'm black you look at me?" Matt said jokingly. Andrew gave him a little, playful shove and they laughed.

"I'm just saying..." Andrew said with a laugh, "If there is some sort of evil ghost there... you might be the first to go."

Colin nudged Matt, "Don't worry man, I got your back!" Then they all started laughing.

Sara really enjoyed her crew. They were as silly as they were serious and worked as hard as she did. But they also brought her out of her head and gave her time to be sarcastic and have fun. She smiled at them. Then she saw a young woman lean over to Andrew.

"Excuse me... Uh... were you talking about going to the Lynch Plantation?" she asked, looking more than a little concerned.

Andrew grinned, apparently not picking up on her trepidation. "Yep! First thing tomorrow!"

The blood drained from her face. "Why... why would you go there?" she asked, her voice shaking.

"See that girl over there?" Andrew pointed to Sara. The girl nodded and Sara gave a little wave. "Well she is a ghost hunter and also a tiny dictator. We go where she tells us," he said sarcastically. A tone this young woman missed.

She looked directly at Sara. "You need to stay away from there."

Sara laughed nervously. "Oh come on... It's just a house. We will be there one night and that will be it."

The young woman looked even more terrified. "You're staying the night?!" she asked. Her voice carried enough that the rest of the people in the café turned to look at them. The soft music in the background stopped playing.

Sara and her team suddenly were the center of attention. Something that Sara was only comfortable with when it was filmed, not live. She looked at all the faces staring back at her. "Yea... that was part of the contract. My team and I have been paid to make a show for it... to raise money to restore it. It will bring more tourism to this town."

"Restore it?" the young woman asked. "We don't want it restored and we certainly don't want any tourists coming here only to be killed by going in that house."

The other patrons in the place nodded their heads in agreement.

"Listen, I have been all over the United States. I have stayed in over a hundred haunted houses. Nothing violent has ever happened and no one has ever been hurt." Sara said, choosing her words wisely. She wanted to tell them that all of this ghost business was crazy and that she had never encountered anything supernatural, but she didn't want that to get out and damage her show's credibility.

"All due respect... you've never stayed in this house." Another guy said from the corner. Sara's crew looked around at the petrified faces.

"So none of you ever go there? Even out of curiosity?" Colin asked.

"The last person that went there out of curiosity was found hanging from the porch the next day." The young woman replied.

"Maybe he was depressed and chose to off himself there." Andrew suggested while rolling his eyes. If anyone was a skeptic, it was him.

"He was my brother," she said. Andrew looked mortified and wished his tea had a shot of whiskey in it.

"Oops," he muttered, wishing he could say more.

"I'm sorry for your loss but we were paid to do something and we never back out of a contract." Sara said while Andrew stared at the table in front of him. "Now, I think we should be going." She said as they all stood up.

They shuffled out of the café and began walking towards the hotel quietly. They were all silently trying to brush off the many warnings they had just heard and get their excitement back.

"It's ok guys, some places just really buy into this crap." Lila offered.

"Yeah... but we have never had that reaction from any other location," Matt said. "Those folks are serious about this shit."

"Come on guys," Sara said. "This is a beautiful, creepy, historic building. It's going to be great, AND safe." They were probably just hazing the out of towners. I bet they're probably in there right now laughing their asses off at scaring us. Well, we'll let them think that way."

"Hey, uh... excuse me! Wait!" They heard someone say behind them. They turned. It was another young woman who had been listening silently in the café. She ran up to them and stopped. "Sorry, its just... we were wondering... who paid you to come here?"

"Um, it's a group called The Conservation Collective of Pre-Civil War Phantasmal Plantations. I believe they support and restore these kinds of places all over the south and have a lot in this area. I looked them up, their headquarters is just on the other side of town next to a Piggly Wiggly on 2nd street." Sara replied.

The girl looked around at the group with a strange expression. "That part of town has been completely abandoned for 10 years. There was a hurricane that destroyed it and we didn't have enough money to restore it... and as far as I know, there has never been a group by that name in this area. And I have lived her my whole life. I really don't think you should go to the plantation... someone is setting you up."

Sara looked uneasy but Andrew stepped forward.

"Listen, we appreciate your concern but I am sure there is a reasonable explanation. No one would spend this much money on a prank. Now tell all your buddies at the café that we aren't backing down."

Sara looked at the girl. If anyone had spoken to her like that she would have just let them walk straight into a moving car. But this girl stood there with panic on her face. She knew she couldn't say more but still looked like she wanted to stop them somehow. Her facial expression gave Sara goosebumps but before she could even consider breaking the contract, Andrew and Colin started leading her toward the hotel.

"This town is full of crazies." Matt said under his breath.

CHAPTER TWO

Sara didn't sleep well that night. The scene in the café played in her head over and over. She lay awake listening to everyone else snoring. Finally, she flopped over to look at the clock. It was 3:19 am. She groaned quietly. She thought about how excited she had been for this and managed to talk herself back into the adventure before her, deciding that the townies just didn't get out much and had possibly seen too many movies. She fell asleep.

By 11am exactly, their van was packed and any trace of hesitation from the night before was gone and the silliness had returned. Colin was shooting footage of their drive on his phone. Sara and Lila were taking selfies with all of the equipment. Andrew was driving, as always and Matt was snoozing in the front seat.

After a 40 minute drive, passing through the town, driving past the university, they finally pulled up to a large flat expanse. There was a dirt road jetting off to the left and a large sign above it that was covered in dust. Matt jumped out and managed to jump up to wipe the dust away. Sure enough it said "LYNCH". Colin couldn't help it, and he jumped out to take a picture of Matt standing under the sign with both hands flipping him off and a huge grin. They all giggled and rolled their eyes. Then they took off down the dusty dirt road. The large house grew as they neared it.

"I knew it was a mansion but I guess I didn't think it would be this big." Lila said.

"What do you think a sorority was thinking in buying something like this?" Sara asked.

"Simple, they could have keggers and ragers without the neighbors complaining." Colin said. He was the only one who had been a part of Greek life. A part of his past he tried to suppress.

They pulled up to the front of the house and climbed out. For a moment they just stood, appreciating its old fashion beauty and its size. It was gigantic. The wrap around porch alone was bigger than Sara's apartment. Sara and Matt continued to look over the house and the land while Lila, Colin and Andrew unpacked the equipment. When they finished, Lila walked up to Sara to make a game plan.

"It's hard to believe that the townspeople wouldn't want to save this place. It's so beautiful." Sara whispered.

"I know. Like look over there! Past that field it looks like there is a pond and small wooded area. And this tree over here would be great for a giant swing..." Lila said as she approached an old Oak tree that was closest to the house.

"Its really big. Like really big. This is going to be our best shoot yet," Sara said.

"Where should we start?" Lila asked.

Sara looked around thoughtfully. "Ummm... let's begin with the civil war history of the plantation and slaves with the fields in the background. Then I will walk to the tree and end at the porch when I talk about the sorority massacre. Got it?"

Lila nodded once and set up her camera. She began rolling as Sara started to talk.

"Hello, today we are in Louisiana at their best kept secret haunted destination. The Lynch Plantation is over 200 years old and has a most interesting history. Built by a Slave trader and his wife in the early 1800s, this plantation was one of the largest and most profitable in the area. Although aptly named for the fate of over 300 slaves, the Lynch plantation actually received its name from the slave trader who built it. James and Mary Lynch became exceedingly wealthy from the cotton cultivated here. Once the war was won by the north, they knew that their way of life would never be the same. Already know to be a cruel master, James Lynch decided that his final act of rebellion against the north was to kill all of the slaves he held. Most of them were hung from the branches of this oak tree but the younger children and smaller women were drown in the pond at the back of the property.

Then the bodies were collected, placed in a pile and burned at the entrance where you can still see bits of burn marks today. Only 5 years after the mass lynching, Mary Lynch suffered a psychotic break, claiming that the ghosts of those she helped kill were haunting her. She stabbed her husband and then hung herself on the porch right here. But perhaps the most famous suicide on this porch was that of mass murderer Gary Lindale. Gary, a maintenance man from the university was hired specifically to look after the needs of this house while it served as the Pi Theta Kai sorority house. He lived in a small servant house that used to stand just over there but has since been demolished. One night, Lindale snapped, much like Mary Lynch and went on a murdering spree killing every single sorority girl inside. He then called 911, left the phone off the hook and hung himself in the exact same place as Mary.

This house certainly is one of our more chilling explorations and we invite you to join us for a night at the Lynch Plantation." Sara said and stopped. That was the cue for Lila to stop rolling. It never ceased to amaze her that Sara could do these on the first take with no notes in front of her. She was a natural.

"Let's say we explore, take pictures and maybe some landscape footage?" Sara asked Lila and Colin.

Andrew and Matt were right behind, having a heated debate about which sorority girls they thought were the best partiers. Sara and Lila tuned them out, focusing on the expanse in front of them. The sun beat down and even in mid-October, the heat made them sweat. For a moment, Sara imagined what it would have been like to harvest in this heat as a slave. She let herself mourn the loss of the hundreds of innocent lives. She didn't believe in the afterlife so she hoped that death was a welcomed rest for them. They explored until the sun got low in the sky.

"Guys we should go inside and set up now." Matt said, turning to the house. They picked up the equipment from the ground outside and walked up the creaking steps to the front door. Lila pulled out a small camera and filmed Sara as she turned the doorknob and pushed. The door gave way with a small squeak. They slowly made their way inside. The entry way was covered in dust but other than that, it looked as though the owners had just stepped out for a moment. There was furniture set up as if company was expected. The long dining room table was set as though the sorority girls were going to sit down to dinner together. They made their way down the hall and through each room. Colin and Lila were shooting footage of everything. Finally they made their way to the living room. It was beautifully decorated and the fireplace even had logs in it ready to be lit.

"Matt and I will set up the cameras in the rooms and upstairs. Lila, you and Colin make sure that the feeds are working and tell us about positioning." Andrew ordered. He was excited. While the rest were busy with their tasks. Sara decided to watch the footage they had gotten before including her intro. She sat on the dusty old sofa and turned on the camera. The footage was even better than she had hoped and for a moment, she was extremely grateful that she had found such talent in Lila. As the video wrapped up she saw the frame of the entire house. Once more she took in the beauty until she noticed something. She paused the video and zoomed in. Up on the second floor in one of the bedroom windows stood a woman in a very old dress staring directly into the camera.

Sara took in a huge gasp of air and blinked. She looked again and the figure remained. She waved her hand toward Lila.

"What is it Sara?" She asked seeing Sara's horrified face.

"Colin, can you see me? How is this?" They heard from the microphone attached to the camera that Andrew was placing.

Lila moved over and looked at what Sara was pointing at. They replayed that part of the video and they were both speechless. They continued to watch through to the end and that was when they saw something even more startling. As Sara had approached the porch and was explaining Mary's hanging, the woman disappeared from the window and suddenly appeared right behind Sara holding a noose. They both gasped in fear.

"That's good Andrew, I think that's the best shot." Colin said into the walkie talkie.

Sara and Lila looked up to see the screen that Colin was watching. The video feed was of Andrew in the same room that the woman had been in in the video. "Andrew!" They both shrieked. Colin jumped in surprise.

"What?!" Andrew said from right behind them. They jumped and turned to him.

"How... you were just..." Sara stuttered.

"There is a 30 second delay. Geez what's wrong with you two?" He asked. They showed him the video while Colin helped Matt navigate setting up a camera in another room on the second story.

Andrew was just as stunned as they were. "I was just in there and there was nothing weird..." He said trying to talk himself down.

Then Lila got an idea. "Colin play back the footage you have of Andrew setting up the camera." She said.

"What..? Why?" He asked confused. He had been too distracted to hear their conversation.

"Just do it." Sara screeched. He did and they saw the room in night vision. It glowed in a soft green and they saw Andrew fumbling with the equipment.

"How long have you been doing this for now Andrew?" Colin teased but no one laughed.

Then just as Andrew leaned over to place the camera and backed away they saw her. The woman was right behind him holding a noose. Colin, who hadn't heard anything before that jumped back and screamed. "What the F***?!" They watched Andrew leave the room and the woman with the noose remained staring into the camera, unmoving. Then finally she turned her head and seemed to float out of the room.

They sat watching the camera in silence until the walkie talkie beeped, startling all of them.

"Colin, Colin! Is this ok? I don't want to be up here alone any longer. It gives me the creeps!" Matt said.

Colin immediately switched the video feed to Matt's camera only to see a close up of his face.

Sara held her breath. She wondered if the woman would appear in that room too. She grabbed the walkie talkie.

"Matt... uh... can you back up so we can see the room." She said with her voice shaking. They watched for 30 seconds and then saw him nod at the camera and back away. Just as they got a glimpse of the room, the feed cut and they heard a thud.

"Matt!" Sara screamed. They watched the screen and saw that it was flashing between black and night vison. When it stopped flashing, it showed something that drained Sara's blood. It was the woman holding the noose and standing next to a tall man in the same period clothing. And at the bottom of the screen they could see Matt's still body.

Andrew and Colin jumped up and ran to the staircase. Lila and Sara could hear their heavy footsteps above them. Lila stared at the screen with a strange expression on her face.

"Wait... that man... I've... I've seen him before. She reached for her laptop and opened it to a bookmarked page. It was an article from a newspaper covering the massacre of the sorority sisters. There were pictures of all 24 victims and a picture of the man who killed them. It was the same man.

Sara and Lila looked at both images in utter confusion. Then the feed from the room was cut completely and just as suddenly, the power went out. The darkness surrounded them and they screamed. In the corner of the room, a giant clock struck the hour. It was only 10 pm but it felt so much later. After the last chime, the power came back on and everything was quiet. Lila and Sara first checked to make sure the other was ok then looked around them. But when they looked at the walls, both felt as though the wind had been knocked out of them. All of the paintings, pictures and decorations were upside down.

They bolted up and ran to the stairway. As they climbed they saw the upside down portraits smiling sadistically at them. That's when Lila first saw it. Blood splatter on the wall. It looked fresh.

"Andrew! Colin! Matt!!??" She screamed and they ran up the stairs.

"Down here." Andrew's calm voice beckoned them to the last room on the right. Matt was sitting on the floor and Andrew was standing next to him. Colin was fiddling with the camera.

"I just told him what we saw." Andrew explained. "He doesn't believe me." Matt was clutching his head.

"What happened? Did they get you?" Sara asked breathlessly.

"Not you too... listen guys this isn't funny ok? My head hurts from knocking it on that shelf and I am not in the mood for a practical joke." Sara was about to try to reassure him that it was no joke when they heard the door behind them creak.

They turned to see a beautiful blond girl standing in the doorway. Her hair was disheveled and there was blood dripping from the side of her mouth and oozing from her sides and arms. "He's coming. You'd better run... although it never helped any of us." She said as her cold blue eyes looked past them to the window.

Then the lights went out again and flashed back on. She was gone and all that remained was a bloody hand print on the door frame.

"Believe me now?" Andrew said. Sara had no idea how he could care about that at a time like this.

"We need to leave." Sara said rushing to the door. But as she ran into the hall, she saw the same man as before wearing modern clothes and wielding a large knife. She saw blood splatter l lining the walls. He was blocking their way to the stairs. She looked around at the other bedroom doors that were slightly ajar. None of them would protect them. Then she looked up. There was a rope that pulled down a ladder to the attic.

"You guys!" She said as she yanked it. The man at the end of the hall started walking slowly towards her, undeterred by her possible escape. They all scrambled up the ladder and slammed the entry way shut before the man with the knife could reach them. They heard nothing. They sat in the dusty attic and silently tried to think of how to escape from the top floor of a mansion without going back into it. Though they were not really safer than before, the attic gave them a false sense of security and they all tried to breathe. Lila looked over at a box near them. She pulled out a very old painting. Though it was dark, she could make out that it was a couple. She pulled out her phone and used the light to look at the image. When she saw it clearly, she nearly dropped it.

It was the same man and woman they had seen in the video. But not only that, the man was identical to the mass murderer who killed the sorority girls 15 years prior. She read the bottom of the frame, "Mr. and Mrs. Lynch".

"Guys…" She said and showed the picture to the others.

"So what was this guy reincarnated or whatever?" Andrew asked. It was strange to hear that from a skeptic.

Just then, the ladder to the attic began to shake. They all looked around to find a way out. There was a tiny window at the other end of the attic. They ran over and Colin broke the old glass with his foot. Sara slid out first and they lowered her on to a part of the roof over the second story. Then it was Lila's turn. When they were both out, they crawled along the shingles to find a place they could climb down to the ground. They found nothing. By time the guys had slipped out, they had found the only possible way off the roof was to lower down into one of the bedroom windows. Andrew went first to break the window and help grab the others. Lila went first, then Colin. When it was Sara's turn she briefly looked around the property and the dirt road. The moon was much brighter than she thought it was and it lit the whole plantation. That was how she saw him. There standing against an old truck was a man, just watching the house and watching them climbing in. He didn't move.

"Do you see that man?" She asked Matt. He looked to where she was pointing and shivered. Something about the man by the truck gave him a sickening feeling.

"Yea… but we can't worry about him right now. We have to get out of here." Matt said.

He helped her lower down then quickly climbed down himself. They all made their way to the door and into the hall. Just as soon as they had stepped into the hall, the man reappeared with his bloody knife.

"Into the rooms!" Andrew screamed and they split up into each room.

They slammed the doors and turned the latches, each praying that the doors would hold from the phantom killer. But no sooner had they each locked the doors when a chorus of screams sounded. Hearing this, Sara turned around to face the room she was in. There was blood everywhere. The walls were covered and there on the bed was the body of a dead girl who had been stabbed over 10 times. Sara let out a cry. She heard the same sound come from Lila in the room next to her. They were all seeing the crime scenes of the girl that had died in each room.

Tears rolled down Sara's face. She ran to the window to try to open it. She would jump if she had to. A broken leg was better than dying. But it wouldn't budge.

"It won't open. They are nailed shut from the outside. He was very clever." A voice said from behind her. Sara turned to see the dead girl sitting up on her bed, the blood still dripping out of her wounds. He lifeless eyes seemed to look right through Sara. Sara screamed and rammed herself against the window. She would break the glass if she had to.

"You'll never make it. He planned this too well. The others that live here are loyal to him. They will help him to kill you. Just like they did for us." The dead girl said. Blood sprayed out of her mouth as she spoke but she didn't seem to notice. Sara tried not to look at her but felt a pulling sensation and her eyes were drawn back to the blood soaked girl on the bed. As soon as she made eye contact the lights went out again then flashed back on. The room was clean and the girl was gone. Then the door swung open. But the hall was empty. Sara poked her head out just enough to see her crew doing the same. They bolted towards the stairs only to see 24 bloody girls standing at the bottom staring up at them.

"He likes the chase. He likes the chase." They all chanted in a haunting harmony. Then they began climbing the stairs. They turned back to the hallway to see the man with the blade and the woman with the noose.

They moved towards them, slowly at first but then began to speed up, disappearing and reappearing closer and closer. Colin panicked and ran into the closest bedroom and slammed the door. Sara could him them trying to break the window. The woman with the noose smiled as she walked right through the door. There was a crashing sound then a thud. Then the door swung open slowly. Lila ran in to see if Colin had made it but as soon as she peered out the window she let out a horrible scream. She saw Colin swinging below from a noose. She turned back to look at her friends in horror but the door slammed shut once more and both phantoms were gone.

Seconds later there were terrible screams and then a gurgling sound. And once more the door swung open slowly. Lila was on the bed covered in her own blood with stab marks all over her body. Her eyes were looking up to the ceiling as if looking a God.

Sara almost ran into her but Matt grabbed her. He turned to look at the mob of dead sorority girls who stood staring with vacant expressions repeating, "He likes the chase."

"Help us!" He screamed. They ignored him. He grabbed Sara's arm and pulled her into the crowd.

"They aren't going to hurt us. They are his victims." He said and he and Sara ran down the stairs. Andrew couldn't move, he was frozen in fear. Andrew had never believed in the supernatural and couldn't process it. Matt and Sara ran to the front door and flung it open. Sara was about to yell for Andrew but at that very moment they saw a body drop from above the porch and swing in the same spot that Mary Lynch and Gary Lindale had hung themselves year before.

"Andrew!!!" Sara screamed. Matt dragged her to the car and fumbled with the keys. Finally he opened the doors and they both got inside and locked the doors. Sara looked at the house, now able to see it clearly in the moonlight. She saw Andrew's and Colin's bodies hanging from their nooses and looked up to the bedroom where Lila had been murdered. In the window stood the man with the knife. Next to him, stood a lifeless Lila. In all of the other windows, the Sorority sisters stood looking out into the night with their dead stares. Matt revved the engine and turned the van sharply to get back on the dirt road. That's when they saw the man with the truck. He stared at them. His gaze was unwavering. After a few moments he got in his truck and turned on his bright lights. Then he revved his engine and slammed on the accelerator. He was driving right at them.

"What the F*** is he doing?" Matt asked in shock. He didn't have time or room to get out of the way and Sara braced herself for the impact. But as soon as the truck would have touched the front fender, it disappeared. Matt looked around and in the rear view mirror. There was no sign of it.

"Just go!" Sara yelled.

And they did. They drove to the police station and told them everything that had happened. The police refused to go to the house until the morning and Matt and Sara stayed in their cell the rest of the night.

In the morning they all went back. It was just as they had left it. The police did their reports and the coroner was called. When they had gotten all their equipment out, Sara asked if they could leave. One of the cops agreed to take them back to their hotel and they climbed in the back of a car. Sara let her look once more at the big house. She looked up at the room where Lila had died. There in the window was Lila looking back at her. She waved a sad goodbye and disappeared.

Sara was institutionalized a week later and this is the only story she will ever tell.

BLOOD STREAM

RACHEL FOX

Of all the days for his luck to backfire it had to be today. The grey light of day matched Wade's mood perfectly. The light haze of rain spattered against his windshield. "Two more blocks, come on already!" His hand came down on the steering wheel in anger.

Wade's alarm had failed to go off this morning, and then his shirt had a stain. From there it had gone downhill. Life was just having a good time screwing him over lately. Downsizing, outsourcing and every other damned excuse had eliminated his job over two months ago. He needed this damn job.

Another red light had him streaming out a litany of cuss words. Finally, he pulled into the garage of Essex Enterprises. A security guard pointed out the level he should park on and Wade began to slow his breathing and regain his grip on his temper. It was now or never and Wade needed it to be now.

Stepping inside the mirrored elevator he studied his image. Wade Carlson was not just another average Joe. He worked hard to stay in shape and maintain the façade of a man put together. His brows furrowed as he noticed the wrinkles in his dark grey suit. Too late to change anything, he focused on the task at hand.

****

Task at hand...what a joke. The prim and stuffy hellion manning the desk at Essex had taken him in from head to toe. Just one godforsaken look to sear his soul and seal his fate. Ten damn minutes had cost him the chance of a lifetime. The beast wouldn't hear any excuses. There were none that mattered anyway.

This had to have been the fastest interview that Wade had never had. Denied; he had been denied even the chance to speak to anyone. His hand fisted at his side as the weight of his briefcase now felt like the weight of the world.

Wade couldn't even stand the reflection in the elevator walls. Everywhere he looked his failure was multiplied and highlighted. Life was one conniving bitch! The ride back into the parking garage seemed to take forever. When a ding announced he'd arrived at his floor Wade dragged his body back towards his small sedan.

His attention was elsewhere. Wade's mind was far from the dark and dank garage. That was the excuse for missing the beautiful woman that appeared from behind the pillar to his left. Even in the darkness of the garage Wade is hit with her beauty. The worst morning has just taken a very nice turn.

Wade turned on his charm and smiled in the woman's direction. Anything attention his way would be a boost to his self-esteem these days. The mystery woman wasn't beautiful, she was stunning. He felt the power of her looks in his gut.

Tall, slender with dark straight hair she could have walked right out of a fashion magazine. Wade felt his palms grow damp with anticipation. He slowed his step to try and stretch out the moment. There was a moment of hesitancy in her stride as she took in his large frame. Wade enjoyed her visual examination.

Feeling brave he stopped a few feet from her and smiled wider. Wade cocked his head to the side and wondered what he'd lead with. Her clean, polished looks didn't bode well for the usual pickup lines. He wanted to make an impression. Women were one of the few things he excelled at.

His mouth opened to speak, but the mystery woman beat him to the punch. Wade watched as she closed the gap between them. The scent of her perfume; soft and spicy hit his nose and filled his lungs. His eyes widened from the intrusion.

Wade whipped his head left and right making sure that they were alone. She was stunning, a dream for any hot blooded male but still something felt off. That prickle of fear people spoke of danced along his spine.

His mystery woman performed another head to toe assessment before she spoke.

"Excuse me, are you Charlie?"

It took Wade a couple of minutes to process her question. He was too busy watching her lush mouth form the words to really hear them. Then it hit him. She was looking for someone and it wasn't him. A pang of loss rang in his chest.

Wade felt sad at the loss of opportunity to get to know her, but was glad that she'd broken him out of his depressive state. So far the day had him at 0 for 2. He began to shake his head when she spoke up again.

"I'm sorry that I'm late. There's no excuse but I just had a situation I couldn't avoid. Are you Charlie? Are you here for the job?"

He listened to her voice. This woman sounded like a leaf in the wind; soft and melodic but looked like sin. Her voice wrapped around his brain and echoed until it clouded his good sense. Wade didn't know why he did it; he didn't care at the moment. The only thing that mattered was the offer she dangled before him.

****

Her skin was pale porcelain against the harsh color of her hair. The wide set doe eyes watched him carefully as she waited for his answer. Wade would have been happy to just remain standing there drinking her in, but the lady was waiting for an answer. The problem was the answer was a lie.

"Don't apologize for being late, as you can see I'm just arriving myself. Charlie..."

He held out his large hand and waited to see if the woman took the bait. Wade wanted her to believe him for two reasons. First he really needed a job in the worst sense of the term. Second, he just wanted to remain in her presence for a little while longer. Selfish all the way around, Wade didn't let himself feel any guilt at the moment.

The slender woman took the last step towards him and closed the distance. Her long, perfectly manicured fingers stretched out and wrapped around his hand. The cool feeling of her skin made a shiver run through his body. Wade mentally scolded himself.

She's just a woman, no big deal. This is the chance to work, get your ass together!

"Thank you Charlie. I was afraid I'd missed you. I can't tell you how relieved I am right now. I feel better about the situation already. Do you have a preference on the location we should talk at?"

Wade wracked his brain and tried to buy himself some time. He had genuinely thought that she worked here at Essex. Never had he thought that this was anything other than that. He didn't even know her name and now she wanted to head off somewhere to "talk". Wade's heart began to race in his chest, but he plastered on a calm smile despite it.

"I always believe it should be ladies first..."

He let his words trail off hoping like hell that she'd fill in the blanks for him. There was only so much time he could avoid using her name before there was suspicion. Wade cocked his head again and tried to seem as unassuming as possible.

What he needed was for this woman to relax and lead the way. Once she started talking and filling him in on information Wade was sure he could take on whatever task she had in mind. Her laughter was a surprise. It didn't match her voice or demeanor at the moment.

The throaty sound seemed detached from the beauty before him. Wade arched a brow and waited for her to open up. He'd never released her hand and wasn't bothered by the fact that she didn't seem to mind.

"I must seem like a fool to you. I swear I'm not Charlie. Nerves, I'm going to blame my rudeness on nerves. Lara, you can call me Lara. I think it's time to move this meeting don't you? If you're comfortable with my choice, I thought we could head to the Montclair a few blocks over."

Wade smiled and nodded his agreement. The Montclair was a large, lush hotel that was the preferred location from everything from power deals to lover's trysts. It was the perfect place to sit and try to figure out what he'd gotten himself into.

"That sounds perfect Lara. I think we should meet there in...let's say ten minutes. That way neither of us has to return to the garage once we're done. For our cars I mean."

Wade didn't want to sound like an idiot, but so far that's exactly what he felt like. He waited for her response. It could go either way and Wade was prepared for either. He'd already lost on chance today, what would one more feel like.

"Perfect. That's a great idea Charlie. I hadn't thought about being seen together. I guess I'm more nervous than I thought I'd be. I'll leave and meet you at the Bronze Bar at the Montclair. I think a private table for two will be perfect. That and a cocktail just might be what we need to get through this."

Lara finally dropped his hand and brushed her hair over her shoulder. After a confident and seductive smile, she turned on her heel and disappeared into the sea of cars within the garage. Wade remained frozen to the spot.

Blindsided was the only word he could think of to describe the way he felt. Who the hell was this woman and who did she think he was? The severity of the situation hit him and Wade began to feel the panic well up again.

He had just bold faced lied to a woman. Face to face, eye to eye he had stood there and let her make assumptions about him. Hell was crowded because of people like him. Wade walked over to his unimpressive car and hit the button for the locks. His briefcase flew over to the passenger seat.

As he slipped behind the wheel Wade knew he had to make his choice; now. It was a two door option and he had nothing to lose at this point in his life.

"Fuck it!"

Wade shouted out loud in the silence of his car. Life was short and he was tired of waiting for his turn to come around. Years of doing the right thing, pulling his own weight had gotten him to this point. All the good had brought him nothing. Struggle, frustration and the lack of what he felt he deserved was all Wade had these days.

The key slipped into the ignition and the rumble of the engine sealed his choice. Wade was done wishing things happened for him. Today he was going to make it happen. It was a short drive to the Montclair, but Wade drove past it. He didn't have the means to valet park his old car and wanted the anonymity in case he needed to make a fast escape.

A parking spot a couple of streets away was the perfect distance to clear his head. Wade lost the tie and unbuttoned his collar. Whatever this woman…Lara had to offer it clearly wasn't stuffy enough for a suit and tie. He debated taking along his briefcase and finally grabbed it before he slammed the door shut.

The alarm's beep sounded loud even on the busy street. His feet hit the pavement and moved straight to the large hotel. The doorman's nod at the entrance made Wade stand a bit taller. He found the Bronze Bar easily and quickly scanned the room for his mysterious Lara.

She sat at a small table hidden in the shade of a pair of tall palm trees. Even in the busy room, she held an aura of mystery and detachment. Wade moved slowly, closing the distance between them. With every step he took, Wade took in all the details he'd missed in the parking garage.

He was no more than a couple of feet away from the table when Lara noticed him. Her back straightened and she smiled at him. Her long fingers stretched out to the empty seat across from hers. Wade settled into the comfortable seat and set his bag on the floor beside him.

"What is your poison Charlie? Tell me what a man like you enjoys."

Wade's breath caught for a moment. This woman was like none he'd met before and the fact that he was in the dark now only made it worse. Behave like an idiot or play her game. He was out of options and stuck, so Wade decided to just play along.

"A man like me? What on earth do you mean by that? Tall? Handsome? Well dressed?"

He tried to laugh at his own joke and hopefully break any tension. Wade's gaze remained trained on Lara's face. He searched for any signs that he'd pushed too far, crossed some imaginary line he wasn't yet aware of.

Lara's throaty laugh reached his ears once again. She smiled and seemed to relax in her seat once more.

"Charlie you are the kind of man that makes a nervous woman relax. The kind of man that I'm glad I took the chance to meet. Please, tell me what you're drinking. Hasn't anyone ever told you that a woman doesn't like to drink alone?"

Her manicured finger traced the rim of a tall wine glass before her. The ruby red liquid gleamed even in the shade of the bar.

Wade felt his old confidence grow a bit. He wove his fingers together as he watched her. Lifting a hand in the air brought a waiter over almost instantly. Whether the staff here was poised at the ready or every eye in the place was on them Wade didn't know. He didn't really care at the moment. The need for the drink she'd offered grew.

"A gin and tonic with lime."

Even with his nerves, Wade managed to sound confident and calm. It was all a lie of course. He couldn't wait to find out what Lara had in mind. More importantly, Wade wondered how he'd be able to take the job she'd spoken of and clear up the misunderstanding.

The tall gin and tonic arrived quickly and Wade raised the glass and held it out to Lara. She lifted her wine glass and tapped it against his highball. They sipped in silence, each of them watching the other over the rim of their glasses.

Wade held his ground and kept silent in the hopes that Lara would lead the way and begin to unveil what was going on there.

"I've heard very good things about you Charlie. It's hard to be taken seriously when fishing around for this type of information, but I guess I got lucky. All roads seemed to lead to you."

He nodded at the compliment, but still didn't say a word. It was a skill that he'd learned to master long ago. No matter what kind of business you were in it was the same. Let the other person talk and eventually you'll have everything you need to make or break them without ever lifting a finger.

People loved the sound of their own voices and were more than happy to spill their feelings when allowed to. Wade settled deeper into the chair and slowly sipped at the cold, tart drink. Every piece of information he gleaned was stored away for later analysis.

"It's a shame that people don't take advice when it's given. I mean we're all intelligent, well-spoken people and yet we refuse to see the truth that's in front of us. Strangers offer their opinions all the time but it doesn't matter. Family...when family offers their opinions you would think that people would listen."

Wade watched the beautiful and seemingly collected woman across from him and wondered what the hell she was talking about. The veneer of polish was beginning to fade and what was left behind was a bit strange.

"I don't have much in my life Charlie. I go home to an empty home and hope that one day it won't be that way. But I do have my family...my brother. He's the most important person in my life. So important, I'd do whatever necessary to make sure he's safe. There is nothing that I wouldn't do to make sure that he remains safe."

Lara leaned forward and fixed her gaze on him. In a voice that brooked no doubt she spoke.

"You do believe me don't you Charlie? Family is everything and anyone who tries to come between a family needs to be stopped. I can't bear to watch someone I know be destroyed. Or worse yet, let them be used."

Wade was finally ready to admit that he had totally misjudged the woman before him. She was beautiful, polished and crazy like a fox. It was time to put this all to rest and make his escape. Wade set his glass down and leaned forward to make his departure.

"My brother is married to a beautiful woman Charlie. Even I am stunned by her; I have been since the start. I was happy for them, jealous even but now...now I feel nothing but distain and fear. She's no good for him. She's no good for anyone."

He was frozen in place again. One look at her and he felt how desperate and serious Lara was. Wade stayed put and waited for her to continue. He had no clue where she was going with all this but curiosity was driving his decision.

"Something hasn't been right for a long time now, but I didn't understand just how wrong they were. Now that I do, I know that I have to do something. Don't you agree Charlie? Shouldn't family protect one of their own? Shouldn't family be the priority?"

****

Wade slipped out of the Montclair hotel in a daze. No matter how many times he replayed the last hour in his mind it still didn't register. There was no way that his life had taken the turn it had. Life just didn't move like this.

He walked towards his car with briefcase in hand. The weight of it seemed bigger than when he'd left the house this morning. Wade instantly knew that his life was changed forever. Lara was walking, talking trouble and she'd set her sights on him.

It wasn't a fair description of the whole situation. Wade had allowed the lie to begin and continue till now. Lara was waiting for him to take action and Wade was lost at what to do next. An hour he'd sat across from her. Wade had listened to her rambles about family and betrayal. She talked in circles, revealing new bits and pieces of the story as she went on.

By the end he was sick to his stomach and doubting everything he'd ever thought. Lara was one hundred percent crazy. Even now, out in the fresh air Wade felt his heart beating in a rapid tattoo. She had made him question everything. Lara had made Wade question the truth.

"You don't understand how dangerous she is Charlie. No one would believe me if I told them, but you do. You believe me because you know the truth. It's not a fairytale or a sci-fi story. I know that they're real. I've seen it with my own two eyes."

Wade shook his head and tossed his briefcase into the car. There was too much pent up energy and nervousness within him to get into his car. He locked the door and walked on. Every step he took had him replaying the conversation in his mind.

Lara's beloved brother was married to a bitch according to her. The man's wife; Kelli was not to be trusted. Not only was she a gold digger, but she was also something more. It was something that Wade could not and would not consider. Lara was off her rocker. Wade shook off the thought; he couldn't even begin to let that train of thought take root.

It took him hours to regain any sense of control. Wade wasted hours until he climbed back into his car and drove to his small apartment. Lying in his large bed he stared at the dark ceiling above him. Sleep wasn't coming and his mind couldn't seem to shut down. There in the dark he finally let the thought slip from his lips.

"Vampire." It was a whisper in the silent room. A trickle of fear crept along his spine. It was all bull. There was no such thing, but still Lara had been so sure. She'd been so hell bent on this "Charlie" agreeing with her that he'd questioned his own beliefs.

Wade swung his legs over the side of the bed and marched into the living room. Sleep was never going to happen, but he needed to do something. Lara was a crazy lady and unless he'd missed something, she was dead set on getting rid of her *vampire* sister-in-law.

He booted up his laptop and pulled out the information she'd slipped him before they'd said their goodbyes. The creamy, thick cardstock felt heavy in his hands. Wade traced the feminine writing.

Kelli Masters

425 Hockner Avenue

She said it was all he'd need to get the job done. Wade typed in the name and address and waited to see what turned up. He wasn't a killer and he sure as hell didn't believe in bloodsuckers, but he couldn't sit back and let this woman live with a target on her back.

Wade scrolled through the information online and thanked all the tech geeks that made finding a stranger this easy. He wasn't prepared for the face that met him. She was stunning in an ethereal way. Honey blonde hair with peaches and cream skin. Kelli Masters was the all American girl that boys lay awake at night jerking off to.

There were mentions of charity work but little else. It seemed Kelli kept to herself. It was barely dawn, but Wade began to prepare for his meeting with an unknowing Kelli. The cool water of the shower helped to fire up his brain cells. He worked the problem out in his head.

"How do you tell someone their sister-in-law is crazy and thinks you're a vampire without sounding like a psych patient?"

Wade was still talking to himself as he out the car in park across the street from Kelli's large home. He sat there for another ten minutes before he worked up the courage to get out. The whole walk to the front door was a comedy of errors. If any of the neighbors were watching he was sure the police were on their way.

****

Kelli Masters' pictures didn't do the woman justice. Wade was still a little off kilter from being this close to her. The scent of her was making him a little crazy. It was something soft and almost sweet. It reminded Wade of a bakery early in the morning.

"I don't understand what you're doing here, or who you are for that matter."

She spoke in a calm voice that had a bit of a rasp to it. It was the sexiest thing he'd heard in his life. Wade tried to focus and sound intelligent, but she was making it damn hard. He cleared his throat and tried to explain again.

"My name is Wade, but Lara...your sister-in-law knows me by Charlie. It was all just one big mistake actually, but in the end it's probably the best thing that could have happened to you. She means you harm and she's expecting me to be the one to bring it."

His hand ran through his hair for the thousandth time as the frustration of the situation set in. Kelli, Lara and whoever this Charlie was meant nothing to him. They were all strangers that had nothing to do with him, but Wade still couldn't walk away.

"Lara...Lara is not the warmest person I've ever met. I'll admit that, but I don't think she would want to hurt me. I don't want to think it anyway."

Wade saw a glimmer of understanding in her eyes and jumped on it. He leaned forward and forced her to look at him.

"No one wants to believe that bad in people, but this is bigger than that; worse even. Lara is not only mad at you, she's crazy. Lara didn't contact me because of money or power, she wants you gone because..."

Wade couldn't make himself say it out loud. He didn't want Kelli to think he was crazier than he was behaving at the moment. There was no way to soften the blow, so he just said it.

"Lara wants you gone because she thinks you're a vampire."

There it was out in the open and this family could hopefully get Lara some much needed help. Wade expected laughter, maybe even offense but he wasn't ready for the momentary look of panic on Kelli's face.

"I was afraid of this. Lara has always been suspicious but I never thought she'd contact someone about her suspicions. You're right about her not backing down. She's like a dog with a bone. It will never stop, not with you."

Lara was certifiable and now she'd placed her brother's wife in the crosshairs. There had to be a way out of this that wouldn't involve him. Wade realized that there was no job worth all this grief.

"You could contact the police or maybe a local hospital. I'm sure that they have a few options for you to consider that would help everyone."

"No, no you don't understand. We can't let this go public, just think of what the press would say. My husband can't afford the scandal and I can't bare the humiliation. Lara thinks you're on her side, but you see the truth. So why not help me? Help me to get rid of her before she ruins all of our lives."

Wade wasn't sure what these women were drinking but he was not interested in any of it. Crazy was running rampant around here. He rose to get the hell out of the house and Kelli jumped to her feet and blocked his exit.

"Wait! Just wait Wade. Let me explain; let me think for a minute. You have no clue what it's been like with her. She watches everything, is suspicious of everyone. My husband may not love me, but we respect each other. Lara is going to ruin all of us."

Kelli's hands came to his chest and grabbed onto the fabric of his shirt. She clung to him and closed the space between them until they were pressed together. Her large brown eyes held his as Wade was lost. The mixture of her scent and the feel of her body made his rational side fly out the window.

"I've been lonely for so long Wade. Lonely and afraid, but now that you're here, I'm not. Please help me. Please just give me a chance to figure a way out of this. You know that she won't stop with you. It's why you came here, isn't it?"

He was beat. Wade knew that Kelli spoke the truth. He also knew that this woman had lit a spark inside him that he'd never felt before. Some job...he was going to be screwed over because he'd woken up late for an interview.

"What do you think I can...we can do? We're not dealing with a sane person. Lara is bound to want proof that you're gone and I'm not in the business of killing or lying. It was chance meeting that has gone horribly wrong."

Kelli smiled at him and laid her head against his chest. She rubbed her cheek across his peck and whispered. Her hot breath had every atom in his body singing.

"A chance meeting that brought you here. I'm just asking you to take one more chance Wade. I can figure it out and then we can be happy. I can make you happy if you let me try."

****

Wade hadn't had to let Kelli try anything. She had proved to him that trying was the best thing in his life. He still didn't have a job; other than killing Kelli that was but he was busier than ever. Lara called him numerous times to meet and discuss how things were going. Kelli called and they planned and plotted and...

Kelli was like a drug. Wade wanted her like his next breath. She was like a bomb that had exploded in his life. Over a week and he still couldn't find his bearings when it came to the woman. Slinking around in the shadows made him feel like a criminal.

Lara was becoming impatient and Kelli continued to ply him with sex to keep him compliant. Wade had lost all control of his life and was feeling the pressure. Women were what got mankind kicked out of Eden and Wade now understood why. Following Kelli around was becoming something he hated.

Having to watch Kelli interact with the rest of the world like nothing mattered...like he didn't exist was too much for him. Wade had never been the jealous type but this woman pushed his limits. This whole situation was spinning out of control.

Wade knew he needed to end it. Losing his job and the security it provided had made him doubt himself, with this whole thing he only felt the doubt growing. He needed a minute to breath, to think. He shifted the car into drive and headed back to his apartment. Time to throw in the towel had come.

Escaping to his parent's old cabin was just what he needed. Silence, freedom and the lack of female attention just might let him get his mind back together. Wade took the stairs two at a time, happy with his new plan. This was just what he needed. It was all going to work out fine.

He fumbled with his keys as he realized if Kelli was serious about them, then she would understand. Wade jammed the key into the lock and pushed his door open. Twenty minutes was all he'd need to pack a bag and lock up. Twenty minutes and he could disappear.

****

The apartment was dark even for the time of day. Wade ignored it at first. Only the movement behind him caught his attention. It all happened so fast. In a flash the door slammed shut and his body pressed against the wall. The cold sheetrock bit into his cheek as someone held him against the wall.

"Hello Charlie..."

The woman's voice carried though his silent apartment. Wade felt his first wave of fear. He wasn't a small man and yet this woman held him immobile. A part of him wanted to fight back, but his rational side took control. She had called him Charlie, which meant that the gig was up. He wondered if she had been sent by Lara.

"What? You suddenly don't like the name? You liked it enough to take it from me. Did you think that I wouldn't find out? Did you think that you could take my job?"

Every question was highlighted by another shove into the wall. His skull felt like a bag of rocks. Any more roughness from her would leave him useless. It was no use fighting her; Wade didn't think he could hurt a woman even if he tried. One last shove had his temple clashing with the edge of a picture frame. Enough was enough!

"Stop it! Just stop for one damn second and let me talk!"

Maybe the yelling wasn't the best idea, but Wade needed her to listen. He struggled against her hold and acted as soon as she lost balance. His arm swung out and slammed her into the wall beside him. As soon as her back hit the wall he caged her in.

"I had no clue the kind of crazy that you were involved in lady. All I wanted was a damn job. Period. Now I've got all sorts crazy shit in my life. Vampires! Really lady!"

Wade was unraveling quick and the real Charlie's reaction to his outburst only made him more confused. She wasn't surprised or confused. In fact she was perfectly aware of the information he gave her. Charlie knew all about the Vampire situation.

"My name is Charlie...so quit calling me lady. The only thing that's crazy is Lara believing you were me. You've had the assignment for over a week. That's ridiculous. You get in and out; it's the only way to stay alive."

She shook loose from his hold and paced further into the apartment. He could see her working through her next move. Wade knew she was dangerous. She had to be. What kind of woman took jobs to kill "vampires"?

"You need to disappear. This is my job, was my job from the start and I'll complete it. If you're lucky Lara will forgive and forget you. If not, I'll find you so don't worry."

Charlie strode towards him headed for the door. Wade reached out and grabbed her. His strong hold held her in place. A mixture of shock and anger flittered across her face.

"Wait, you don't think that I'm actually going to let you kill Kelli, do you? She's not a damn vampire and both you and her sister-in-law are insane."

Charlie was small but fast. Wade's brain took too long to understand what was happening. She had him pinned to the ground in a flash, her knee pressed into his neck. Charlie played with him, cutting off his oxygen over and over.

"I am a vampire hunter and you need to mind your own business. Human life is precious to me; if it wasn't you wouldn't be breathing right now. I am going to walk out of this apartment now and you will forget all about me and those women. Go back to you little inconsequential life Wade; let the big girls handle the monsters in the dark."

Charlie pressed into his neck once more until tiny spots danced in his vision. Wade heard his door slam shut before he dared to move again. He knew in that instant that he was royally screwed and worse yet; Kelli was in danger.

****

It took Wade all of ten minutes to figure out he couldn't just ignore the danger headed Kelli's way. He didn't dare call to warn her. Wade didn't know who or what this Charlie woman was and he didn't want to tip her off.

Clearly Charlie knew enough about him to find where he lived. Wade called in a favor and borrowed a friend's car. He slipped behind the wheel of the 4x4 and headed straight to Kelli's home. He parked down the street, just like the first time.

Wade sat in the truck and watched the street. Darkness had fallen and the entire neighborhood seemed silent. Nothing seemed out of place, but Wade really wasn't sure about that. Sneaking in and out of Kelli's home the past week had left him little time to really investigate his surroundings.

He'd spent the last week thinking with the wrong head and it had cost him. Wade had lost himself in Kelli and stopped thinking straight. Temptation wrapped in smooth, soft beauty. The truck's door sounded like a bomb when he shut it.

Wade crept across the lawn and circled around back. He tried to sneak in the same way he did when they had their trysts. The hair on the back of his neck stood at attention. Kelli was a virtual stranger and yet he needed to know she was fine. Wade needed to see her and hold her to reassure himself that everything was still fine.

The door to the garage was unlocked and the lights were out. Wade moved silently through the house searching for any sign of Kelli or even that pathetic husband of hers. Wade would never admit to anyone how much he wanted to see the man right now. This was all his fault; his and that crazy sister.

Voices came from the front of the house and Wade changed direction and headed that way. He kept his body close to the wall and listened closely before taking each new step. The closer he got, the clearer the voices became. Kelli and...Charlie were arguing in hushed tones.

"How many years...centuries even did you think that your evil could stay hidden? Even if you did keep it hidden by such a lovely skin."

"You have no clue what you're doing. That pathetic woman thinks that she has all the answers but neither of you truly does. Listen to me and you might just live through the night."

Charlie's laughter rang through the quiet house and made Wade shiver. There was something so evil about her tone. None of the conversation made any sense, but he knew that he needed to get to Kelli...now.

"Don't spew your charm to me monster. I'm immune to all your lies. It's my job, my destiny to make sure that your evil is exterminated. You see Kelli; it's going to be my pleasure to watch you take your last breath."

Wade felt real fear then and charged into the room. He tried to charge Charlie but again she proved him overconfident. Charlie spun and landed on his back. She used Wade's momentum to force him to the ground. Their bodies twined together as they rolled around wrestling for control.

They banged into furniture and sent glass and picture frames crashing to the floor. Shards of glass pierced his skin, but he didn't relent. The sound of blood rushing in his ears blocked out everything else. Wade used all his weight to try and pin her down.

Charlie rolled them over and straddled his chest. Small and fast and one hundred percent confident, she reached into her boot and pulled out a long thin blade. The silver gleamed in the light and held Wade frozen.

She waved the blade in the air. Wade could see the glee in her eyes as he tracked its movement.

"Look at him Kelli. Look at what your control has done to him. Just one more man who's succumbed to the whims of a monster. It's sad really. He seems like such an intelligent and capable thing, too bad he's going to have to die."

"Wait! You know that it's not necessary. You have what you want. You have me. The great Charlie; the huntress has caught her prey. Leave him and let's finish this."

Kelli's voice rattled in his brain. She was going to save him. Save him by giving herself over like a prized calf. Wade couldn't let that happen. He struggled under Charlie's weight for a second before everything went dark.

****

Lara's voice filtered into his head. The sharp tone made Wade's body jerk. It all came back. The images of earlier rushed back into his mind. Kelli...he needed to find Kelli. She was going to be hurt or worse...killed.

"Kelli..."

"Did you do it? Did you kill her? Tell me Charlie...damn it tell me!"

"She's here, they both were." Wade forced himself to sit up as he blinked to clear his vision. His head snapped right and left looking for any sign of Kelli. But all he saw was a disheveled Lara.

Wade shoved her out of the way and began to search the house. They had to be here. He had no clue how long he'd been out but she still had to be here. Lara followed him, yammering on and on about nonsense.

"Where are they? Tell me Lara!"

He watched her come to a stop before him and look at him in confusion. She was useless. Just as he turned to leave she spoke.

"What do you mean...they? You were hired for a job Charlie. You were supposed to take care of Kelli. It should have been simple for you. Everyone said so, you're the best. Now tell me what happened to her. Is she dead?"

Wade lost control and grabbed the slender woman and tossed her against the wall. Charging towards her he pinned her by the shoulders. He was panting by now; his harsh breaths fell onto her face.

"I am not Charlie you bitch! I want to know the truth, right now. Lara why did you want her dead? What the hell is all this shit about vampires really about?"

Lara's eyes widened but she didn't show any fear.

"You lied to me and sealed your own death in the process. That vampire shit you're talking about is all real whatever your name is. Your lovely Kelli is one; she's one of the most powerful ones around. She made promises and I fell for them, but I guess you know what that feels like."

Wade was breathless. None of this could be real. It just wasn't possible. All of these women were bat shit crazy. He clenched his jaw as he tried to stay in control, but Lara pushed on. She just couldn't shut up.

"I didn't lie about my brother. He has it all; my parents didn't think that I should inherit much. Daddy said that's what husbands were for. I don't want or need a damn husband. Kelli understood, she agreed that we were better on our own. With Marcus gone she would get everything...we would get everything."

Wade couldn't help but laugh. Lara was indeed crazy, now she had added greedy and heartless to the mix.

"You think I'm stupid but I knew it would never work. Once she got it all, that monster would get rid of me. She didn't think I had it in me, but I did...I do. I had to get rid of Kelli so that I could finally have what was rightfully mine! I'm still going to get it; no one is going to stop me."

She had gone from crazy to certifiable in an instant. Wade felt sick by the whole thing. Not only had Lara used him, but now he believed that Kelli did too. His hands released her like she was on fire. He couldn't wait to wipe them all out of his memory.

Wade took one step then another widening the gap between them. Lara watched him carefully. It took her a second, but she bounced back into action.

"I have to find them mister. I did my part and now Kelli must die! Marcus is gone and now it's her turn. It's the only way this works. Where did they go? Who took them?"

"Charlie has her and from what I saw I'm sure she's taking care of her as we speak. Where? Who the hell cares? Just as long as it's far away from here."

He turned to leave but Lara caught his arm.

"Wait, just wait for a second. You and I we can still win here. Help me, help me find her and make sure she's gone and I'll make it worth your while. I'm asking you to help me and I will guarantee you a million for your trouble."

****

One million dollars; it was the price Wade had sold his soul for. He sat in the driver's seat of Lara's expensive Mercedes and followed her directions. Crazy or not; she had a plan. Using Kelli's cell phone, they were tracking her last location.

Wade's hands were damp where he clenched the steering wheel. No matter how he tried to spin this knowledge in his head all he knew was these women were evil. Evil and crazy. It wasn't the money, well not solely that made him agree.

A part of him still wanted...no he needed to make sure that Kelli was alive and well. Even if he knew they would never be or stay together, he needed to assure that she was in one piece. The car slowed as Lara pointed out the small warehouse to the right.

"It says she's there. It looks like no one is around. This is perfect. One, two, three and all our dreams come true. Come on Wade, our future is waiting."

Lara was out of the car before he'd pulled the key from the ignition. She stumbled forward on sky high heels without a care for the danger that could lurk here. Wade hung back and watched their surroundings.

He'd been up close and personal with Charlie and knew the woman was deadly. If crazy Lara had a death wish then so be it, but he was leaving in one piece if he could manage it. The door to the warehouse squeaked loudly in the night. Lara didn't care; she just pulled it open and stepped inside.

Idiot! It was the only thought that Wade had as he watched her storm inside. He waited another few minutes and listened for any sound of struggle, but all was silent. Slowly, cautiously Wade made his way closer to the warehouse and what he was sure was his doom.

He didn't make it nay father than five feet inside before the women's voices reached him. Wade was almost afraid to breathe and give up his location. If they were all focused on each other, then none of them were thinking of him.

"You double crossing bitch! Did you really think that you could get away with this? You really have no clue what kind of power you're dealing with."

Wade watched Kelli's mouth snarl in fury. The woman he saw was not the same one he'd bedded this past week. Gone was the sweet, soft and compliant woman he'd made scream over and over in ecstasy.

"Why is she still alive? Can't any of you do the damn job? I did mine! I got my hands dirty and got rid of Marcus...now it's your turn!"

Kelli's eyes widened in shock. Wade guessed she had underestimated her crazy sidekick. Charlie stepped into view with a long silver blade. It shone in the circle of light as she waved it around in front of her. The assassin ignored Lara's hysteria and focused only on her captive; Kelli.

"Day in and day out my only joy is ridding the world of another of you monsters. Hell, I would do it for free but there's always someone out there who'll pay. This is one paycheck that I am happy to collect. Actually, I think it should be the men I'm saving who should be paying me."

He watched as Charlie continued with her little speech and ignored Kelli. She had been bound to something overhead, but now she was free. There was no way to describe how quickly she moved, how silently. It felt like forever, but in only a matter of seconds Charlie had been brought to the ground.

His mouth opened on a silent cry. Charlie's blood sprayed through the air as Kelli sliced her throat open. Lara finally realized what was happening and began to scream. In a blink Kelli was before her. The same hands that had caressed him now held Lara's face immobile.

"You should have trusted me my sweet. It would have been better for you if you did. Money is nothing more than a game to me. Lifetimes of winning and losing it and it no longer matters to me. Now it's all mine, well mine and Wade's. Right my love?'

Wade stepped further into the space, into the light. He couldn't comprehend what was happening. The terror in Lara's eyes didn't seem real to him. Wade watched as she placed a single kiss to Lara's head and snapped her neck.

With every step closer she took Wade felt the bile rise in his throat. They were all right; Kelli was a monster.

"I'm so sorry you had to see that my love. It wasn't what I wanted. But now we're free. You and I can start over, be whoever we want to be."

Wade took a step back from her and saw the displeasure written all over her face.

"What are you doing lover? This is no time to run. This is our start."

Another step back widened the gap between them. The flash of anger couldn't be hidden by Kelli any longer.

"This isn't what you want to do Wade. I'm offering you the chance of a lifetime. I'm offering to make your dreams come true."

He shook his head. There were no dreams with Kelli, only nightmares. Another step to the side made it obvious Wade had no desire to be anywhere near her. He searched the space around him for anything that could help.

Kelli charged towards him and Wade reacted before he could think it through. Charlie's blade lay at his feet. A stumble backwards brought his hand to the hilt. It wasn't heroic or vengeful. Piercing Kelli's chest was pure instinct and survival.

The howl of pain was something he'd never experienced. The weight of her small body was greater than he'd expected. It was a long time before he could move again. Wade lay there as the life seeped from her small body.

****

The sunlight cut across the room as the sea breeze wafted in in from the deck. Exhaustion hung on him like a sweater. Wade cradled the mug of coffee in his hand as he wandered outside. The nightmares were still there, probably would be for a long time.

He'd earned the cancelation prize Kelli had left him. A hundred times over in his opinion. Wade looked over the railing of the deck and smiled into the steaming mug. His muscles were sore, but they only proved he was getting better.

With his back turned to the sun he let his eyes wander inside. The blades of steel shone in the sunlight causing him to close his eyes. Wade smiled with a deep satisfaction.

"Now it's all mine, well mine and Wade's. Right my love?"

Kelli's own words had sealed his future. The vampire had put the wealth in his name just as she'd said. It's hard to control that much money when you lived for centuries. With all of the crazy women in his life dead and buried; Wade Hansen was a multi-millionaire.

Money wasn't everything and Wade had learned one important lesson. Monsters were real and he wasn't going to be afraid any longer. Wade Hansen had found a job. He was the new vampire slayer in training.

SHE WOLF

It happened again. The same dream. She was sprawled outside atop the wet leaves. Her shoes were missing. The rain was starting to mist down, and everything was wet and earthy. Mud stained her clothing. There were curious red stains beneath her fingernails. The same dream, arising from nowhere, disturbing her sleep.

Anna checked the nightstand, where her alarm-clock stared back at her: six a.m. Early still. Grant would be waking soon. Her husband lay beside her, leg wrapped around the blue duvet cover, mouth partially open while he slept. She resented that mouth. She disliked the way it drooped slightly in his sleep, but she came close to hating it when he was awake. True, he had always been faithful. She had to give him that much. There was no other woman in Grant's life; rather, he had an ongoing affair with his career. The conversations, arguments, and casual remarks of the past ten years had been shaped around work. Nothing was ever enough. There were no good mornings that were not mornings of closing the deal—of progress—whatever "progress" was. He had always been ambitious, but in a keen, hungry sort of way—the type that plowed over bystanders. Once he had flattened them, they were easily ignored.

Anna's face was wrinkled in an expression of partial disgust, and she turned on her side, still damp from sweat. Soon, she would have to get out of bed—would have to begin the morning exercise of making herself neat and tidy for the office, of pounding on bedroom doors to rouse her teenaged sons, of struggling to have a cup of coffee in the morning chaos. This, she realized, was not what she had envisioned for her life. She *tried*. She made the best of it. She saw a therapist and exercised and followed the health advice of morning talk shows ("Cut down on red meat and eat your leafy greens!"). She gardened. Most of the time, however, Anna felt like a husk: something withered, something angry and small. The feeling never seemed to go away. It nicked her ankles, shrouded her, wrapped itself in her stomach and waited. Beside her, Grant let out a low snore. He twitched. She frowned.

As a child she had wanted a big house and a kitchen full of light and sound, a family to tend to and to watch over, and she had wanted it with the sort of fierceness that came from not understanding herself: an intense desire to love because she had wanted to badly to *be* loved. She had the kitchen, and certainly it was large—large and modern, equipped with appliances, filled with food. She did not fear hunger or the cold. Her bills were paid on time. She had no real debt to speak of. She had achieved the dream and found it utterly lacking. She had gotten her big house, but it felt as though very little love resided there. She did not know, sincerely, if she loved her husband. She felt no passion for her occupation, and her children regarded her as a dictator at best. Most of the time, Anna was *noise*. Anna was simply *there,* occupying space. She sat up in bed, and Grant buried his face deeper into his pillow. She had been having the dream for months now, and each time she had awoken from it, she had found herself unable to fall back asleep. This time was no different, and so she decided to go downstairs, to watch as the sun came up and cast its orange-red light on the world. As she peered through the blinds, she found it was raining gently outside. *So much for the forecast,* she thought.

"Heard you've been having one hell of a time with the Morgan house, eh?"

Todd Closterman, a mustached real-estate broker, her superior at the office, tapped his pen against her desk as he passed. His face had an expression of faux-concern that she found off-putting. He wore a tie that had tiny, powder-blue anchors on it, though she was certain he never sailed. He was a golf man. He practiced his swing in his office, but never with an actual club. An air-swing, sometimes delivered after finishing a phone call, sometimes after a bit of motivational advice. *Send it soaring,* indeed.

"Remember, you're doing more than selling the property. You're selling the dream," he said, chuckling a bit. Anna bit her tongue.

"The *property* requires a lot of repairs. The plumbing will have to be completely overhauled. I doubt anyone has done anything with it since it was first installed," Anna replied. "It's not attracting a lot of interest, Todd. There aren't many people looking for fixer-uppers with all the housing developments popping up around here. You know, homes with functioning outlets and clear water."

Todd waved her comments away. "Yes, but that place has charm. Sell them on the charm."

Anna sighed internally. It was possible that the property, a late Victorian-style house plucked straight from a Faulkner novel—all narrow hallways and scratched wooden floors—had been charming when first constructed. Now, it had too few cabinets and not enough space for wall-mounted televisions. Or so she had been told, countless times, by clients.

"I'll do my best," she said, a bit curtly, and Closterman nodded.

"Keep on your leads, too, Anna. Network, network. It's all about networking. You've got to know people to *show* people."

Anna promised herself that if she made it through the rest of the conversation without visibly rolling her eyes, she would leave early. She'd stop and get a bottle of merlot on the way home. A present to herself for putting up with the—

"Oh, Kyle, hey—" Closterman had caught sight of the part-time intern, a gangly twenty-year-old taking courses at the local community college. Closterman had appointed the poor boy to the coveted position of non-fat latte retriever and glorified copy-maker. At least he was distracted. At least she could return to her work. Two more hours and she would leave. She could make it. *One breath in, one breath out.*

At home, the lights were off. The boys were over at a friend's (or so they claimed) and Grant was staying late at the office. He'd sent her a text rather than calling, and it had simply read, "Late again, dinner with Phil." Phil was his pink-faced coworker, a fellow investment banker prone to drinking his meals at the corner bar. Anna had only met him a handful of times, but it had been enough to form an impression. She responded with casual acceptance: a text simply reading, "All right." She put her phone and her bag on the counter, nose wrinkling as she sniffed the air. The garbage, in the corner, had been neglected. Jordan and Shaun, her boys: the incapable duo. Well, maybe they had been in a rush. Teenagers were forgetful. She threw away the brown paper sack that her bottle of wine had been carried in and proceeded to tie the trash bag. "Thanks, mom," she mouthed to herself.

Outside, the air was cool and damp. Paper-thin yellow leaves littered the gutter and the driveway, and they stuck to the bottoms of her shoes as she walked, garbage bag in hand, down to the end of the blacktop. Her footsteps made a wet *thwick-thwick* sound as she moved. In the distance, she heard the muffled noise of car horns and engines, but they felt very far away, almost as if their mechanical groans were being sifted through damp cloth. Streetlamps trailed alongside the rows of partially-lit houses, casting a sickly sort of light onto parked cars and fences, creating shadows that stretched farther and more aggressively than they should. Anna shivered and kept walking.

As she approached the garbage bins, she detected, beneath the odor of damp pavement and rotting trash, something very strange. A muddy, sharp sort of smell—the scent that animals gave off when they had been in the rain. Sweat and fur. Dirt and oil. Her eyes scanned the line of parked vehicles to her right, but there were only tail-lights and license plates. She sighed, but the scent remained. It filled her nose, growing stronger, choking her. Her mouth tasted of it. Her stomach turned. She quickly lifted the lid of the garbage bin, heaving the bag into it, and as she lowered it, she caught a flicker of movement in her periphery.

Something slow and hulking moved under the cloak of a nearby elm tree, but it made no noise. Anna stood frozen, watching, trying to make sense of the shadows playing in the dim light. She wanted to turn, to run back to the house, but her legs felt sluggish. Useless.

From behind a parked sedan, it prowled. *A dog, some sort of large dog*, Anna thought. She backed away slowly. Its fur was matted and dark, patchy in places as though lost in a fight or possibly from disease. *Rabid* flashed across her mind, and she remembered seeing a rabid dog once, sometime as a teenager, as it ran across the park, snapping, growling. She had watched from a nearby shopfront, waiting for animal control to arrive. It had been a yellow Labrador, and when it ran, its jaw had hung open, tongue exposed, eyes vacant. This animal was not a Labrador.

It was canine, but larger than a dog (*closer to a wolf*, she thought) but that made no sense. Wolves didn't live in Ohio; they certainly didn't invade suburbs and slink behind Honda Civics. *A zoo, maybe it recently escaped...or maybe it wasn't a wolf at all.* It moved gradually, almost with purpose, and its eyes caught the light of a streetlamp and flickered, greenish-yellow, in the darkness. Everywhere, the smell of wet fur clung and hovered, and beneath it, something coppery, something like metal. Anna was still retreating, almost hypnotized, when it saw her. It bared its teeth: long, somewhat yellowed. Sharp. And then, spotting her where she stood beside the garbage bins, it growled.

Anna did not run, because running meant chasing, and chasing inevitably meant *catching*. She tried, desperately, to step calmly backward, moving up the driveway in small steps, her shoes making the same smacking noise on the damp leaves. The animal followed, and in the darkness it looked monstrous. Its back was arched, raised high with tension and rage.

I'll get to the door, and I'll go inside, and then I'll call animal control. I'll be having a bath and a glass of wine in no time, she reasoned, but the animal's bared teeth seemed to mock the idea. Her chest hurt terribly, and she realized she had been holding her breath. As she exhaled, trembling, the animal snapped at her, and its jaw made a low, clicking sound as it closed. It paced closer to her, and she saw clearly the raindrops gathered on its fur and the scruff of its chest. It was injured and angry, and it was moving toward her, snarling.

In the distance, a car engine backfired, and the animal lunged wildly. It swiped long claws against her hip, tearing her skirt, digging into her skin. The force knocked her onto the ground. Anna was vaguely aware of yelping—not quite a scream, but a sound of sharp pain and surprise—and she felt her body connect with the wet blacktop. She raised her arms to shield herself, waiting, shaking. She imagined a thousand times what it would feel like when the animal's teeth sank into her arm, but the bolt of needle-like pain never came. She sat, one arm covering her face, for an eternity, and when she inhaled, there was only the smell of wet grass and rainwater in the air. She lowered her arms, looking around rapidly, panting. There was nothing, save for quiet homes and empty cars. Her skirt was torn, and she was bleeding where the claws had shredded the sturdy wool. The blood stained the torn fabric and her skin, almost ink-like in the limited light of the streetlamps. There was no animal in sight.

"I know what I *saw*, Grant," she seethed, phone to her ear. "My skirt—it tore my *skirt*. You can figure out dinner for the boys when they get home. I am not taking chances on this. I want to see a doctor. Who knows, it could have been rabid, it could be *diseased*. You can boil water for pasta. You can handle that, at least. What? *Fine*. Tell them to order a pizza." She ended the call abruptly, cutting off the sound of her husband, and threw the phone into the passenger seat.

The hospital was quiet when she arrived, and several hours later she left, headed for home, with a fresh rabies vaccine delivered to her hip. It stung as she drove in the darkness, and on the radio, the disc-jockey played jangling, up-tempo oldies. "Cruisin' and a-rollin, with my gal," sang the honeyed voice of some presumably now-deceased doo-wop star, "Rockin' and a-jiving, all over town." She shut the radio off and drove in silence, wincing and exhausted. And when she reached her home, she went directly to bed and slept, pulling the blankets around her.

She dreamt of running, and the ground beneath her felt like it was caving in. There were animals fleeing somewhere ahead of her, and she could smell them. Her body moved quickly, powerfully, and the only sound was the sound of her own breathing.

The morning sunlight was sharp. Anna's eyes felt unfocused, and her head pounded. Grant had already left for work, leaving the bed empty beside her. She swung her legs out of bed slowly, wincing as she stood. Her feet were sore and tender. In the bathroom's artificial light, she looked tired. Gray. Carefully, she re-bandaged the claw marks on her hip, where the skin was torn and angry. A purple bruise had blossomed around the area and was once again covered by a white gauze. Anna had taken the day off, planning to spend it in solitude. Perhaps she would read a book in silence or make herself a hot cup of coffee. Her stomach, however, did not approve of coffee, and somewhere inside, she felt a restless sort of feeling, as though she had somewhere to be or something she ought to have been doing. She attributed it to nerves. *And never having a break,* she thought. *Face it, Anna, you're overworked. You never have time for yourself.* And so she went outside, walking into the backyard—a quiet, fenced-in lot with a wooden gate that opened into a small thicket of trees: a green space in the cramped suburbs. She moved with care, trying not to cause her fresh wound greater pain, but trying to satisfy the urge to do *something* with her time. Beyond the backyard gate, within the thicket, she let out a long breath. It was cool, and the October air rustled the tree branches above her.

A bird landed on one and began to chip, sporadically at first, and then, it continued. It was high-pitched and whistling—a shrill sort of sound that broke through the late morning air. Anna ignored it, surprised at her own irritation, and walked onward, smelling the damp soil beneath her feet and observing the mossy rocks and fallen twigs. The bird flitted to another branch, closer this time. Its song was piercing. Its small black eyes focused on the ground, then the sky, then back again. Anna waved an arm, hoping to frighten it, but the bird remained. Her head was aching, and the noise was too much. Her fingers twitched. She realized that her shoulders were tensed, pulled up higher and closer than they ought to have been. She was angry—angry at the invasion, angry at never having a moment's peace. Without thinking, she grabbed a wet stone from the ground and flung it at the bird. She wished, for a fleeting moment, that it would hit the bird—knock it down. *Hurt* it. But the stone missed, soaring just past the dark brown body, making a dull thud in the distance. *What is wrong with me?* She wrapped her arms around herself. The bird had finally flown off, and Anna walked slowly back toward the house, shaking her head. She had never been so quick to anger. She had never wanted to hurt a living thing.

The days passed slowly at work, and she spent most of them in a daze, unable to concentrate. The sound of papers rustling and the incessant ticking of the clock on the far wall made her feel ill. When her coworkers ate their lunches, the smell overwhelmed her. Chili or last night's vegetable stew microwaving, spinning, being consumed by mouths that never fully closed—the sound of a spoon clicking against someone's teeth. It was repulsive, and she began to feel, somehow, that her coworkers were repulsive as well. Their cologne was cheap, their clothing carried the scents of their homes, of their most recent meals, of car exhaust or pets. Their skin was sallow under the fluorescent lights of the real estate office, and their conversations were always the same: baseball tryouts, cookouts, bridal showers, babies, buyers. It never ended. More than once she had gripped the pencil in her hand so hard that it had cracked. She'd tucked the broken pieces into a drawer, glancing around to make sure no one had witnessed. She felt trapped. Caged. When she had been younger, in her twenties, she had smoked a pack of cigarettes a day, and now, she felt like taking up the habit again, if only for the smoke breaks. When she prepared dinners at home, she did so methodically, paying little attention to whether Grant and the boys ate, rarely eating herself. Grant was fixated on the company's latest merger, rambling on his phone constantly about shareholders and assets, speaking a language she detested—the language of business. Jordan and Shaun were preoccupied with the NFL, blaring the television from the living room nearly every evening, knocking over bowls, never apologizing, never cleaning. *Did they eat their dinner?* Truly, she did not know. She simply scraped the abandoned plates with a fork and dumped the waste directly into the trash, not bothering to store leftovers. Her hip ached, and she was due for another round of shots. *Maybe it's the shot,* she mused, clearing the dinner table one evening, *making me feel so strange.*

She began taking walks in the evening, roaming, almost-dreamlike, through the neighborhood. She watched as people went about their routines, always undetected as she passed by illuminated windows. When she tracked in dead leaves or traces of mud, the boys complained but never cleaned it up, and she let the dirt of the outside world sit on floor until she felt like dealing with it. Once, Grant had cursed and blamed Jordan and Shaun for the mess, but if they had denied it, if they had pointed to her, she did not know. She had not been paying attention.

On a Sunday morning, the house was quiet. The boys were sleeping and would continue to do so for hours, and Grant was away on a weekend business trip to Chicago. In the bright kitchen, she stood looking out the window, watching as a squirrel darted from the fence to the grass, running across the backyard. It made a winding and erratic path through the leaves, leaping onto the bird bath and then down again once more. Her stomach rumbled. When she had woken, trudging into the bathroom, she had noticed that her eyes were bright. They shone in a way that was almost feverish, but she did not feel ill. She looked...more *alert*, somehow. As though she had slept more deeply than she had in years, as though her worries had lifted. Internally, she was still fighting a restless, roaming feeling, but she had to admit, the mirror had told a different story. Now, watching the morning activity of her backyard, she put a hand over her stomach as it rumbled again. She walked to the refrigerator and pulled it open, scanning its contents: butter, orange juice, grapes, onions. On the bottom shelf were two strip steaks, waiting to be prepared. She had bought them last week, but had not gotten around to fixing them. They were intensely red, marbled slightly with stark white fat. She poked a hole in the plastic wrap, pulling it into a larger tear with one finger, and reached for one cut with her bare hand. The meat was cold and thick, and she held it up, smelling it. It had a rich, iron scent. Anna, standing in her bathrobe, began to eat the steak. In the silence of the kitchen, juice and blood dripped onto the white tile.

"Something is happening to me," she whispered, looking into the rearview mirror of her car. If this had been a horror movie, she would have been sprouting fur and howling, but it was not. She sat with her hands in her lap and examined her reflection: brown hair pulled into a loose ponytail, soft crow's-feet around her eyes, and Yves St. Laurent lipstick staining her lips. But no fur. No fangs. She sighed and tried to laugh at herself, but it came out like a coarse sort of groan. She had driven to Lake Erie, hoping to stroll along the waterway, hoping desperately to clear her mind. That morning, she had broken a ceramic mug in frustration while trying to get Jordan and Shaun out the door, ushering them to school, ushering them *away* from the house. It had shattered against the pantry door, navy and black shards that had once formed the words "Kennedy Space Center" and now resembled a mosaic. She had not called the office that morning, and she was not convinced it truly mattered. They wouldn't miss her. Closterman would have his comments when she returned, but that was fine, he was an endless source of comments. The boys had stared at her, glancing from the broken mug and back with a look that said, "Crazy," and after they had slammed the front door, she'd watched them walk down the sidewalk with a feeling of rage that made her insides ache. *Crazy.* Maybe she was.

She had considered a hundred possibilities. Stress, mental breakdowns. Rare flus. Anna had called her therapist, but her once-regular appointments had dwindled over the past year to monthly visits, and there was simply no room for scheduling before November. Shots—it could still be the rabies shots. Perhaps they had unusual effects on her. Perhaps she was experiencing a completely new set of side effects. Perhaps she should tell the manufacturers of the vaccine. They could write articles about her. She would be a valuable research subject. The doctor had told her that her vitals were normal, that she looked healthy, and that she had no reason to worry—*simply keep scheduling the next shot.* "You're nearly done with the whole ordeal," he'd said, trying to reassure her. The "whole ordeal" was just beginning, she felt. Her hands shook at any irritation. Her ears were sensitive to noise. She couldn't even watch television. The radio was out of the question, particularly the station that played advertisements for car sales to bad-credit buyers. Everything was noise and color, and everything was intrusive. When Grant slept, she thought about screaming, listening to the sound of his snores, dreaming—undoubtedly—about foreign investments and whatever else caught his fancy. When he brushed his teeth in the morning, she hoped he would accidentally scald himself with the hot water. She hoped, all the time, for silence.

The breeze coming in from the lake was cold, and it picked up her hair and blew tendrils of it around her face. She walked for some time, watching the boats move lazily across the expanse of dark water, listening to the sound of waves lapping against the shoreline. When she got back in her car, her hands were stiff and aching, and she turned on the heater, warming them up by blowing on them. Her body was shaking.

The drive home was a little over an hour, and the sun, after making a rare appearance, was beginning to set. Brilliant crimson and gold cascaded over her surroundings, illuminating them, making them shimmer. The heat of the car and the hum of the engine made her yawn, and the yellow road lines stretched out as far as she could see, one long strip of paint, reaching out into eternity. She began to imagine that she was driving through a great and sprawling forest, and around her were ancient pines and furs, blocking out the noise of the world. Their dark green masses reached skyward and filled her nose with the scent of growth and comfort, a clean and stringent sort of smell that calmed her, lulled her.

At some point, she became aware of flashing lights behind her, and in her reverie, she imagined them to be the sun's rays shining through tree boughs, but slowly, she realized they were the lights of a patrol car: red and blue, following, howling. She panicked and blinked, jerking slightly in her seat. The car came to a stop, and the patrol car's tires made crunching sounds as it slowed over the gravel behind her. Anna turned off the ignition and waited.

She let out a breath and glanced up at her rearview mirror, waiting to see the officer emerge from his vehicle. What she saw was her face, smiling—more than smiling, it seemed to *snarl*. She stared at her own eyes in the mirror, horrified, and they flickered in silent laughter, a dancing laughter. *Those are not my eyes. That is not me.* She grabbed at her face as the officer tapped at her window. *Please don't let him see. Please don't let him know. What is happening to me?*

He was a young man, stocky, and he leaned down with a look of suspicion on his face, but his expression held no indication of surprise.

"I was following you for a while," he told her.

Anna's heart was racing with a sickening speed. Her tongue felt sticky and dry. She cleared her throat.

"I'm sorry, really," she replied. "I must have been dozing off. It was careless of me. I should have pulled over."

"Have you been drinking tonight, ma'am?" he asked, reciting the same questions he surely asked of any erratic driver. But Anna felt judged, irritated. She clasped her hands.

"No, of course not. I'll perform the test, if necessary. I've been ill, and I wanted a bit of fresh air. I must have been more tired than I thought," she responded. "I'm fine now, though."

She spoke quickly, anxiously. Anna hoped her face was not twisted into the grin she'd seen in the mirror. She could not tell. She ran her dry tongue over her lips.

The officer took her license and went back to his car to run it, and she sat, window rolled down, the cold air blowing in waves across her face. *Drive off,* her gut screamed. *Leave him sitting there, stunned. Stunned like an idiot. Drive away.* She shook her head, trying to clear her thoughts. When she looked in the mirror again, she saw the face of a familiar, nervous woman. Her face was pale, her eyes wide, but at least it was a face she recognized. The officer let her off with a warning and a lecture, and she thanked him, rolled up the window, and sat watching as he drove off. She'd told him she wanted to collect herself.

Anna felt the corners of her mouth twitch. Her lips curled upward, ever so slightly, barely exposing the top row of teeth. She let out a strange, tittering chuckle. She was only dimly aware of the sound, but it filled the quiet car, bouncing off the dashboard. In a daze, she raised a hand to cover her mouth, pressing it against the source of the laughter.

"They've called me three times, Anna," Grant was saying. He stood in the kitchen, gesturing to his phone almost comically, his eyebrows raised. She had entered the house only moments ago, but had little memory of arriving home. She stood, shielding her eyes from the kitchen light, feeling slow and confused. Grant was pacing, and he pointed to the phone again.

"I was in a meeting and forgot I had it on. It rang when I was on an overseas conference call. Do you know how that looks? It looks irresponsible. Why haven't you been at work? Two days now, is it?"

Anna shrugged, disoriented. "I've been sick."

"And where have you *been* all day? Look, Anna, I covered for you. I told them it was an emergency, that you had forgotten to notify them, but I can't take calls all day from real estate offices. Anna, have you considered that they might *fire* you? Are you seriously ready to lose a job over this? Over that stray dog?"

"It wasn't...I don't know what it was. But it wasn't a dog. It was something else," she murmured. *And it's inside me*, she thought, almost smirking. Grant was not listening. He was ranting, and in the living room, the boys had ESPN on loudly, shouting at the sportscasters. Her mind was spinning. And somewhere, the laughter was bubbling up inside her. Somewhere, a snarling, giggling sound was building.

Grant paused, looking at her with narrowed eyes. "Are you *on* something?" he asked.

"And what would I be *on*?" she countered.

He frowned, dismissing the idea, waving his hand in the same way Closterman waved his hand. Dismissive. Irritated. As though to say, "Your problems are not *my* problems, Anna."

"He's going to have to step it up if he wants to break that record, though," the television blared from the living room. Anna's mouth twitched again.

"It's not like you, Anna," Grant said. "It's like you're just not..."

"What? Here? Am I just not 'here'? Am I somewhere else?" Anna was on the verge of giggling, but her heart was pounding. Her skin shone with a thin layer of sweat. She wiped her brow. "Does it matter where I am?"

Grant made a noise of frustration. "To hell with it. Don't have them call me. *Tell them* not to call me. Work it out. Make up something to tell them but *don't* have them call me."

"Sure," Anna replied. "Can do." She glanced around the room, and her eyes were unfocused. The ceiling light looked like a fat orb, hovering motionless over the granite kitchen island. Grant grabbed a beer from the fridge, shutting the door with a smack. It rattled the contents of the inner door, a sound of glass on glass.

"I'm going downstairs," he told her.

"Sure," Anna repeated. She watched him go down the basement steps and, when he was out of sight, headed to the bathroom. She stood watching her face in the mirror. Feral eyes, lit up and wild, stared back at her.

When she woke the following morning, there was mud on the floor. She didn't remember how it got there. She didn't remember leaving.

"We're heading out," Jordan called from the bottom of the stairs. The boys had organized a camping trip—the last weekend of the season to do so—and were staying overnight with several friends whose names she only vaguely recognized. She was at the mirror, and her mouth was pressed into a thin, hard line. She bit her own lip. It turned white under the pressure of her teeth, and soon, the force punctured the delicate skin and began to draw blood.

"Mom," Jordan repeated downstairs, and she heard Shaun say, "Whatever. Let's go."

"Have a good time," she called out. Red curves dotted her lower lip. The thin line of her mouth shot upward. A curved smile.

"We might not have reception," Shaun said.

"That's okay. Be safe," she said, and her shoulders shook. She listened to the soft rustle of their backpacks bouncing against their bodies, the sound of their footsteps and the door opening and closing below her. They had left the television on downstairs, and it was running promos for the nightly news.

"An important source of calcium you *might* not guess. We'll tell you what it is, coming up tonight," a perky, female voice said.

Anna left the mirror, walking down the carpeted hallway toward the stairs. She ran her hand along the wall, letting her nails drag against the textured paint, flakes accumulating beneath her fingernails.

Another promo.

"Cold fronts moving in signal a chilly end to October, and be sure to catch the full moon outside tonight—you'll have a pretty clear view," a man's voice casually informed the empty living room. "More on tonight's weather."

Anna descended the stairs, hand trailing on the banister. She reached the television and turned it off, and then walked, head tilted slightly to one side, toward the kitchen door. No noise. Perfect. No sounds. No television.

She went into the backyard and stood on the cold stone patio, where the patio furniture sat abandoned and unused and her gardening equipment had been left to gather rainwater. Her thick gloves were lying on the stonework, and she reached over, brushed her fingers against them, and tossed them onto a nearby gardening bench. They rested there among empty clay pots and trowels. She walked across the lawn, and stopping midway, removed her shoes. The grass was damp and soft beneath her feet, and she made long strides across it, sinking her toes into the earth. In her back pocket, her phone began to vibrate. She ignored it.

Anna stared up at the sky, watching the gray clouds roll slowly across her vision. From somewhere very far away, she recognized the sound of Grant's SUV pulling up in the driveway, the slow roll of its tires, the abrupt silence of its engine. She perked her head, listening as the door slammed and he headed toward the house.

Her phone began to vibrate again, and this time she accepted the call, holding it away from her face and staring at the caller i.d. as it lit up the screen. The office.

She could barely make out the sound of Todd Closterman, his voice coming across the line in an impatient sort of way, trying to sound good-natured, trying to sound like a buddy. A pal. Her pal, Todd.

"Look, Anna. Are you there? Anna? If you're there, it's Todd at the office. We need to talk. I'm not sure we can keep your position—" His voice cut out as she dropped the phone on the ground, smiling a wide smile. Her tongue ran across her lips. A copper taste. She could hear him continue, softly now, muffled by the ground, "—need to discuss how to move forward from here."

Grant was inside by now, and she moved gradually back across the lawn, feet wet from the grass, toward the gardening bench. Todd's voice trailed off as she put more distance between herself and phone, and soon, she could not hear him at all. Anna's eyes traveled over the bench.

A clear view of the moon. A clear view of the sky.

She picked up a pair of gardening shears, feeling their weight in her hands. A solid feeling. They smelled like metal and dirt. Through the kitchen windows, she could hear Grant on his phone. She waited until he had finished his call, until silence filled the house again. A big house. A modern house.

Anna's lips were a snarl—an animal smile.

A clear view of the moon.
She carried the garden shears into the house.
END

A MURDER NEAR PERFECT

STEVE SAXON

Chapter One

The paperwork in this job was what would eventually kill him. Jack Morrison was convinced of it.

He had an endless supply of fresh reports to review and sign, and acquisition forms to fill out, and personnel files to oversee. Of course, that was the way it went once you became CEO of a successful company like Evergreen and Howe. He'd been years getting to this position. He wasn't going to complain now about a little paperwork.

Not with the other perks his position came with.

It was already two hours after normal business hours but Jack wanted to make sure all the other people in the low-rise skyscraper in the heart of downtown went home before him. At this point, he could be fairly confident of his privacy. It was Friday, after all, and normal people all went home to their wives or friends or their television sets. He had a wife to go home to himself, but there was no rush. Besides. Jack was not normal.

He was superior.

In a world of perfectly adequate men and boring examples of the male species he rose above them all. He was better than the rest, which meant he was above the laws of normal, polite society. What he desired, he got. What he wanted, he took.

And right now what he wanted was waiting for him on the other side of his office door.

Pushing aside the neatly stacked folders that had—in all honesty—been finished half an hour ago anyway, Jack pushed the intercom button on the phone at the corner of his desk. When it buzzed, he said, "Miss Hollis, come in here please."

"Yes, Mister Morrison."

Her voice was like warm honey. His blood stirred just to hear it and know that at any moment...

She walked through the door, one leg at a time, wearing that tight black pencil dress that he'd been staring at all day long. She had always been a strikingly beautiful woman. Blonde and built like a Victoria Secret model, toned and tight where a woman should be tight, and soft and supple in every other way. With exaggerated slowness, Veronica Hollis folded herself into the chair on the other side of his desk. Her eyes held his gaze with smoky intent while she folded her legs. Her dark stockings slid smoothly against each other as her skirt rode up her thigh, and she let her one high-heeled shoe dangle.

"What can I do for you, Mister Morrison?"

His heart thumped and the trousers of his business suit were suddenly too tight. A wicked grin slid over his face and he leaned forward on his elbows. Was there something she could do for him? Yes, there certainly was.

"Take your clothes off."

The steam in her eyes became a raging wildfire that spread from her to him in pulsing waves as she arched her back to reach around and undo the zipper of her dress. She wasn't wearing a bra. Damn, but she wasn't even wearing panties under her stockings. As he watched, she rolled them down her legs, one at a time, stretching out in the chair in ways that were impossibly suggestive.

As she twisted her hips on the leather chair, her fingertips crept up her legs, drawing his eyes and making him have to loosen his tie to unbutton his collar. It was suddenly very hot in here.

"It's your turn, Mister Morrison," she said to him, her voice husky with need and her scent filling his nostrils. Her perfume. Her sex. Her heat. "Time for you to strip, you big, bad boy."

"You don't tell me what to do," he scolded her.

Unfolding her legs, Veronica tickled her own skin up higher, and deeper... "I said, undress."

Jack smiled. It turned her on to be in control. Well. He could let her be the one to be in control for now. As long as he got what he wanted. Her.

As he undid his shirt, and stood up to tackle his belt and the zipper on his trousers, she languidly rose and met him. Their lips touched. Their hands explored each other. Impatiently, she pushed his shirt down his arms, and then stripped his pants down to his ankles. On her knees, in front of him, she eased his cock out and stroked him hard and kissed him tenderly.

Jack eased into her caress and let her bring him up close to his edge and back again, and then up to his edge once more. He was master of his domain. He had taken this woman for his lover just a few months after hiring her. He deserved this. His wife was for home. She was fine, for a woman in her forties. She took care of the house and made sure he looked good in public, but Veronica was fifteen years younger. She was hot blooded and frisky and capable of doing the freakiest things in bed. Or on the floor. Or in the shower.

She was in his life to make him happy, and meet her needs. That's all she was good for. Of course, the way he felt right now, it was well worth the money he spent out to maintain a wife and a mistress. She was—

"Leave your wife," she told him.

He blinked down at her, lying under him on the couch in the corner. They were both of them so very close to going off that it was almost painful but now her words made him lose the feeling altogether.

It wasn't the first time she'd demanded this. He put her off time and time again, but she was becoming more and more insistent.

"Now isn't the right time," he said to her. "When it is I will—"

"No," she told him, her hand sneaking in between their bodies. "Now. Leave her now. For me."

"Veronica, it's not—"

"Now." Her hand teased him.

"I said not now."

"And I—" She did something that jacked his senses up to eleven. "—said now."

"Veronica..."

"Now. Do it for me now or this ends."

Her hand stopped moving, and he gasped for breath and squirmed against her, trying to make her touch him like that again.

"I can't just leave her. Not now."

"Do it."

"I..."

"Do it."

"Veronica, please...!"

"Do it!"

Her hand moved, and he rushed up and over his climax.

"All right!" he screamed. "Yes! Yes I'll do it!"

"Tonight," she said, making one final demand. "Do it tonight."

He was barely able to think after what she'd done to him. All he knew was that she'd made him promise to leave his wife. In that instant, he would have promised to turn the whole company over to her if she'd only keep doing this with him. It was just sex...

Only, it wasn't. This was something more. He hesitated to use the word love, but it was as close as a man like him would get.

This was what he wanted.

Chapter Two

Jack pulled into his driveway a half hour later. He parked his Lincoln Continental, a powerful car for a powerful man, and stepped out. Then he hesitated. Inside, his wife would be waiting for him and he was here to tell her it was over. They were splitting up.

Only, the thing that he'd never told Veronica was that his wife and he had a prenup agreement. If he left her, she got half of all his money and more than half of his assets. He would no longer be the powerful man he had become accustomed to being. He would be just like everyone else. Would Veronica even want him after that? She was with Jack Morrison, CEO and wealthy lover. When he wasn't those things, everything with her would end...

Leaving his wife would mean losing Veronica.

Inside the house, Jack listened to the silence. Maybe Maria had gone to bed already. Maybe he was off the hook for the evening. He could always go to work early and not have to deal with his wife and his lover until tomorrow morning.

Then he heard the soft splashing from the tub upstairs and realized that Maria—his wife—had gone to take a bath before bed. She did that sometimes, and then she came to bed squeaky clean and smelling of soap and nothing could be less attractive to him than the sight of his naked wife in her curlers without her makeup. They hadn't been intimate in weeks. She was starting to be suspicious of him but he really couldn't care less. He was getting what he wanted at work.

He climbed the spiraling staircase to the third floor and went down the hallway to the bathroom, walking as if his feet were encased in cement. When he pushed open the door, Maria looked up at him from her tub full of bubbles. She squinted, and twisted her mouth up in that sour frown she wore so often. "Well. You're home late."

"I have a very important job," he told her. "you know that."

"Maybe you should concentrate on being important to me."

Bile rose in his throat. If any of his employees ever talked to him like that he'd fire them on the spot. If any of his competitors ever talked to him like that, he'd mount a hostile takeover and run them into the ground.

So he was supposed to just take this from his wife?

He took a step closer to the tub.

"Oh good," she said to him sarcastically. "You can scrub my feet for me, since you're staying."

She lifted one leg up over the edge of the tub. Her feet were wrinkled, and the toes were crooked, and Jack hated her feet. She knew he hated her feet.

Come to think of it, there wasn't a single aspect of her body that he did like.

He came closer, and she picked up her wine glass from the edge of the tub and drank from it. "Why don't you just go to bed like you always do, Jack? You're boring me. In fact, I've been bored for the last ten years. We never do anything anymore. Why don't we do something tomorrow? Just you and me? You are still my husband, right?"

Was he?

"The foot brush is over there."

Was he really her husband?

Looking down at her from the side of the tub, he reached down with both hands.

"What?" she asked him.

He never answered. His hands were already around her neck and he was pushing her down under the water. She struggled, and he pushed harder. Those ugly, ugly feet of hers kept kicking him in the chest, leaving wet footprints on his shirt. When she pushed her head up over the water he slapped her again, and again, and again, until she slipped under the bubbles again and he held her there.

It was a long time later when he realized she wasn't struggling anymore.

Jack stood up. His hands were shaking but it wasn't because he was upset or nervous. His muscles were still spasming. They were cramping.

He'd squeezed her neck so hard that his shoulders and his arms ached. He'd never killed anyone before. He stood there now staring at her and he had to wonder. Was he supposed to feel anything? Shouldn't he feel sad, or angry, or...evil or something?

He didn't. He felt free.

With a deep breath he turned away from her. He needed a drink. A good stiff cognac maybe. Something that was fitting for a man as worthy to be free as he was. He turned to leave the bathroom.

And stopped.

In the mirror, his wife Maria stared at him with hatred in her brown eyes.

She lifted a finger and pointed directly at him.

Jack whirled back around to the tub. Maria was not standing there. She was lying dead in her bath water. But he'd just seen her...

He looked back at the mirror. It was just his own reflection. Just him.

Nerves, he decided. That was all it was. He'd just killed his wife. Of course he was going to see her face. He might even see her in his dreams.

While he was in bed with Veronica.

He smiled at his reflection. Life was good.

This was everything he ever wanted.

Chapter Three

"Where are we going today, lover?"

She always called him lover now. Three weeks after his wife's unfortunate accident in the bathtub, when Jack had come home to find her dead and had tried everything he could to revive her. He'd tried so hard. He was distraught.

At least that was what he told the police.

In private, in bed, he and Veronica congratulated each other on their plan. Just talking about it turned her on. Jack talked about it every chance they got, when they were alone together, in private.

It was a gorgeous weekend morning now, and Veronica was asking him what they were going to do. He'd already taken her skiing in Sweden and yachting around the Cape of Good Hope. Last weekend they took a mountain hike in the Adirondacks and at the top of some rinky-dink mountain called Azure they had stripped each other down there in the trees and screwed each other until a troop of girl scouts had stumbled on them.

So what were they doing this weekend?

"I thought we might hop the company jet to Hawaii and spend a couple of nights there," he told her, sitting up in the bed next to her and very purposefully caught the blankets on the edges of his fingers and pulled them down, revealing Veronica's perfect, firm breasts. She smiled at him, twisting suggestively. "Don't start that, now. If we get...physical with each other there won't be any time to take a plane."

"To Hawaii," she yawned.

"Not impressed?"

"Mmm. Sure. Hawaii sounds nice."

She actually sounded anything but impressed. "If you want to do something else just tell me."

Reaching over to wrap her fingers around her thigh, she turned that smoky look of hers on him. "What I want to do is you."

"As much as I like the thought of that—"

"Shut up," she told him, rolling over on top of him, straddling his waist, pushing her hair back over her shoulders and rocking on him roughly. "You aren't leaving this bed today."

Well, well, well. He liked the way she said that. He liked the thought of—

A shadow flashed by the door to the bedroom.

"What was that?" he said, putting a hand on her stomach to hold her still.

She took that hand and slid it up over the mound of her left breast. "It was my heart. Feel it? Feel that...? Mmm. Yes. Right there."

"No, I mean out there."

He squinted at the hallway, where the morning sun was bright and showed him that there was nothing there. He relaxed and let what Veronica was doing to him heat his blood and flood his mind. She was so good at turning him on. So good at using her body to make him forget about the entire rest of the world. Besides that she was completely insatiable. He really believed that she meant to keep him in bed here, all day, giving him sex like no woman had ever done before.

Suddenly he found himself thrusting and pushing, sweating and breathing hard as his hands clasped her thighs and around to her ass. He was into this. All the way into this.

Opening his eyes he looked up, expecting to find Veronica looking back at him with that little half-smile that she got on her face right before she found her release. Her face swam into focus—

Into the angular and puffy-eyed face of his dead wife.

He may have screamed. It was hard to tell in his haste to push away from the woman who was clawing at him, demanding he stay with her, calling his name. He pushed her away, and fell on his ass to the floor next to the bed.

"What is wrong with you?" Veronica demanded, kneeling at the edge of the bed to look down at him, holding a hand to her shoulder where he had hit her hard enough that a bruise was surely going to form. "Seriously, Jack. What the Hell was that?"

"I saw...I saw..." He looked behind her. He climbed up on the bed and looked past her and over the other edge and God help him he looked under the bed as well. There was no one else here but him, and Veronica. "I don't know. There was...you were...Maria."

Veronica's face turned sour. "You saw your wife?"

He felt so foolish. "Yes."

"While we were making out just now, you were thinking of your dead wife?"

"Of course not! I don't think about her. Ever."

She sat back on her heels, crossing her arms under those perfect breasts. "But you saw her. What was she doing?"

"She was..." Having sex with me, was what he was about to say. He bit his tongue down just in time. "Watching us."

There was a moment of silence as Veronica's eyes grew wider. "You saw her here, in our bedroom?"

Jack didn't know how to answer. Yes, he saw her. This was her bedroom before it was Veronica's, so shouldn't she be here? But...she was dead. She was gone.

How could he possible still be seeing her?

"Forget it," he finally decided to say. "It was nothing. Just a trick of the light, I'm sure. Sorry. Really, I'm sorry."

He reached out for her but Veronica pulled away from him. "I'm going to take a shower," she said, her eyes still wide. "Let's just forget that happened. Okay?"

"Yeah, sure..." She was already gone into the adjoining bathroom. Jack sat down again heavily on the edge of the bed, staring all around him. There was still so much of Maria in this room. In this house. It had only been three weeks since Maria's death of course. Still, maybe it was all of her things, all of the little touches that she'd put into this house, that were reminding him of her. That must be what had just happened. That's all it was.

So tomorrow he would hire an interior decorator and get the entire place redone. Make it entirely his and Veronica's. That's what he'd do. Getting up on his feet, putting the nonsense of the past moment behind him, he took his dressing robe off the back of the doo and wrapping himself in it to head downstairs and find some breakfast. The household staff had the weekends off so it was just him and Veronica in the house. Have to make due for themselves. Thankfully he was a master with a skillet and a carton of eggs.

In the kitchen he found everything he needed, from frying pans to eggs to freshly chopped red and green peppers left for him by the housekeeper. Setting a pat of butter into the pan to melt, he leaned back into the fridge for the glass carafe of milk. He hummed a little tune as he picked that out, along with an onion to add to the omelets when it was time.

And when he turned back from the fridge, Maria was standing right there, pointing her finger at him, her mouth open in a silent scream.

His scream was anything but silent. The milk dropped to the tiled kitchen floor and shattered into thousands of glass shards, thick white liquid flying out in all directions. He stumbled back, fragments of the carafe biting into the flesh on the bottom of his feet. Red now mixed with the white stream flowing into the tile grout.

Jack fell on his ass and quickly rolled to his knees to crawl around to the far side of the center kitchen counter. He hid there, pulling his knees up to his chest and shaking so hard that his teeth were chattering. It couldn't be her. It couldn't be Maria. He had to be hallucinating it. Yes. That's what it was. Maria was dead.

She was dead!

When he finally got the nerve to push himself up and look over the edge of the counter, he saw Veronica standing there, in a pink robe of her own, a towel wrapped around her hair as she patted it dry. Her eyes took in the floor, and his frightened face, and her mouth hung open in a little round "o."

"What happened?" she asked him.

Nothing, he wanted to say. I'm seeing things, he wanted to tell her. It was nothing, he thought to add, I'm just worked up because I killed my wife and maybe I feel just the tiniest bit guilty over that. Maybe.

Only, in the back of his mind he began to wonder. This was twice—no, three times now—that he had seen Maria after her death. He knew for a fact that there was no one else in this house but him. Only him, and Veronica. So if he was really seeing Maria, if he wasn't crazy, then there was only one explanation.

Jack stood up, careful of his right foot where there was still a triangle of glass stuck in the pad of his big toe. "Nothing happened, dear," he told Veronica with a wide smile. "I just slipped and stepped on some broken glass. Why? What did you think happened?"

She smiled at him uncertainly, and then went back upstairs to get dressed. Jack narrowed his eyes at her as she left. He enjoyed having Veronica in his life. She was good for him in a lot of ways. She was the best sexual partner he'd ever had, that much was for certain. He liked that she was in his life.

But...

Someone was making him see his dead wife. Someone was playing games with his head. If it was just the two of them in this house, well.

Veronica was up to something then, wasn't she?

Chapter Four

Monday he was at work again. There had been no further incidents with Maria since Saturday morning. He almost gave up his idea that Veronica was somehow trying to make him think he was crazy. Only, it made sense. He was a strong-willed, confident man. He knew where he stood. He knew what he'd done in his life was worth more than a dozen other men combined. He was not the sort to fall victim to hallucinations or have guilt make him go half crazy.

No. Someone was doing this to him, and that someone was Veronica. He was certain of it.

All morning long he played the part of the good company employee, making sure reports shuffled across his desk in good order, and that all of his tasks were seen to. He smiled at Veronica, who was still his personal secretary, and complimented her on her work, and even found reasons to touch her lightly on the back of her hand or the side of her neck. She liked things like that. He was going to play the devoted and doting boyfriend until he knew what she was up to.

His suspicions, of course, fell to her wanting his fortune. By killing Maria and making it seem like an accident he'd managed to keep all of his money and his assets, from the mansion on the hill to the beach house in Maui, from the two million in stock options here at Evergreen and Howe to the quite valuable stamp collection that he had kept since he was a kid. It was all his. This was a common law state, however, and if he died then any woman who could prove that she'd been living with him as his significant other would be in line to inherit all of that herself. There was ample reason to make him think he was insane.

Or worse, kill him.

That was why when Veronica brought him his afternoon coffee, he didn't touch a sip of it. When he ordered his lunch he made sure it was from a place that delivered so that she wouldn't have any excuse to go out and get it herself. He would be cautious about everything he did with her, until he knew the truth.

Which was what his three o'clock appointment was about.

"Mister Smith, your task is very simple." The man sitting across from Jack was not named Mister Smith. That was the name he used to keep his own anonymity in situations that were this delicate. He was a private detective, and the check that Jack had already written was made out to Mister Smith's company, Magic Eyeball. It was a lot of money, and Jack expected to get his money's worth. "You are to follow Veronica for me for the next few days, and find out if she is cheating on me, or if she has any evil intentions towards me."

"Evil intentions?" Mister Smith parroted. "You serious? That's a pretty big word for what I do."

"You know what I mean."

"I do," Mister Smith assured him. "Consider it done."

When they went home from work, Jack couldn't help checking his rearview mirror over and over, trying to spot the tail he was sure Mister Smith had put on him. The man was good. Jack never saw anything.

At home again, Veronica said she had a headache from the long day at work and went up to bed. Was she planning something? Could this be the night when he caught her in the act? If so, he wanted to give her plenty of time to hang herself. Mister Smith was probably already watching them through the windows with high-powered cameras, or maybe his company had already bugged the house. They did that in the spy movies, didn't they?

"I'm going to go out," Jack told her as she started up the stairs. "I'll send the staff home as well so you won't be disturbed. How does that sound?"

She smiled at him, and winked, and Jack smiled with her until her back was turned. Then his face turned to stone. His love for her was slowly turning to ash, and he knew in his heart that he was right. She was trying to get at his money. That's what all of this had been for. He couldn't trust her. He couldn't let his guard down around her ever.

Once Mister Smith had his evidence of what Veronica had been up to, he wouldn't need to keep his guard up. He could get rid of Veronica, too, and move on to someone else. He wouldn't even have to do away with her himself, like he had Maria. Just kick her out. Yeah. That's all he would need to do. Then he could move on. There was that pretty young girl in the mailroom who looked like she wouldn't mind moving up in a new position. Like underneath him, on his couch...

Licking his lips, Jack grabbed his coat and stepped outside to his car. There really wasn't any errands that he had to run but at the same time he wanted to be away from the house to let Veronica think she had a free run of the place. Let her do whatever she would, and let Mister Smith catch her! If he was lucky this would all be over tonight.

The Lincoln's engine revved like a well-fed kitten as he raced down the lonely stretch of highway west of the city. The windy road, and the trees, and the emptiness helped him clear his head. He felt far less paranoid now that he was alone. Veronica had him so twisted up in knots that he couldn't see straight but out here, by himself, he was free again. That's what mattered. He was free...

Adjusting the rearview mirror he caught sight of the face, of the woman sitting in the seat behind him. Maria smiled, and Jack lost control. He screamed. The car veered to the left, over the wrong lane, into the trees and then out again as he wrestled it back onto the pavement. The tires bit into the asphalt and spun the whole vehicle around and Jack was absolutely certain he was going to crash and die before the side of the Continental slammed up against a stand of young trees and with a horrifying, wrenching sensation deep in the pit of his stomach, the whole world went still.

Breathing heavily, scared more than he'd ever been scared in his whole entire life, Jack looked into the rearview mirror again.

Nothing. The backseat was empty, as he knew it would be.

Then he put the car back in gear. It took him a few tries to rock the vehicle out of where it was stuck and put it back on the road. He drove very slowly, very carefully, with his hands on the wheel the whole time. It took him twice as long to get back as it should have. He didn't care.

Veronica wasn't here. She wasn't here in the car with him. He was all by himself. Which meant Veronica wasn't the one making him see his wife. No. This was far worse than that.

He laughed at himself. It started out small, and then got louder, and uncontrollable. He laughed until he couldn't stop laughing.

He was going insane.

Chapter Five

Jack tried to call Mister Smith's cell phone over and over. There was no answer. He left one voicemail. Then another. "Mister Smith, it's me. Again. Veronica isn't...she isn't the one. This is something else. Please call me. Please."

Inside the house, he found a note from Veronica. It said she had gone out with friends and would be back later. Nothing unusual in that. She went out to spend his money all the time. Usually he didn't mind. Now, he knew that he wouldn't be able to get rid of her because it wasn't her pretending to be his wife. It wasn't her making him crazy.

It was him. He was the one going insane.

He started to laugh again, but made himself stop. He had to get ahold himself. He had to be the strong man he knew he was. The leader among men. The strong, dominant male, who always—

Behind the kitchen island, on the tiled floor, he found the body of Mister Smith. He was laying there with deep purple bruising all around his throat, his eyes bugging out of their sockets, his face pale and his lips blue. He'd been strangled to death.

"No…"

He went to kneel down next to the man, to examine the body, when he heard the water running in the upstairs bathroom.

For a moment he stood there frozen, staring up at the ceiling. The water, in the bathroom. Just like the night Maria died.

The night he killed her.

One step at a time, very slowly, he went up to the bathroom.

The silence was deafening as he stepped inside the room. The bright lights shone off the white linoleum and the fixtures. In the oversized tub water lapped at the sides. The faucet was no longer running. The bubbles floated on the surface and the steam from the heat of it rose into the air. It was just like that night only there was no body. No Maria.

He stepped closer. He could hear the beating of his heart. He could feel every nerve in his body jangling like his skin was on fire. Nervously, sure that he was going to see Maria lying in the water and waiting for him, Jack leaned over the side of the tub.

It was empty. There was nothing there.

He pulled in a deep breath and slumped against the tub. There was nothing wrong. It was just water.

Whatever hit him across the shoulders was heavy enough to knock him off his feet and into the bath. Water splashed everywhere. Pain blossomed up and down his spine from where he'd been hit. He swallowed soapy bubbles and gagged and swallowed some more and then he thrashed until he was facing up and he could get a breath of air again. It hurt to breath. It hurt to think.

It just hurt.

When he opened his eyes she was standing over him, holding a length of metal pipe and smiling at him in that way she had. She advanced on him, one leg at a time.

Veronica.

"How are you, Jack?" she teased, slamming the pipe down on his hand as he caught hold of the edge. The sound of bones breaking echoed in the space around them. "Are you having fun today? I sure hope so. I've gone to a lot of trouble to make this fun. Well. Fun for me, anyway. You probably aren't having much fun yourself."

Jack held his hand to his chest. His clothes were weighted down with water and he could hardly move at all but he knew, somehow, that if he didn't get out of here that Veronica was going to kill him. She was going to take everything he had.

"Did you like my little games?" she asked him. "I had that mask of your wife made up special. I wore it in the bedroom that time we were fucking each other. Then later, down in the kitchen when you thought you saw her and you dropped the milk? Yeah. That was me as well."

Maybe, Jack thought, she would tell everyone that he'd gone insane. Drowned himself the same way that he'd drowned his wife.

"Then in the car," she went on, smiling and laughing at his pathetic struggles to keep from falling under the water again. "Did you like that bit in the car? It's an inflatable doll that I put that mask on with a remote trigger. You know? So I could inflate it from here. Then, deflate it right away. Nice trick, right? It's pretty amazing what money can buy."

"I'm...not crazy," he said more to himself than to her. "I'm not crazy! You did this to me. You did this to me, you bitch!"

Her beautiful face darkened. "Now, I don't much like that word. You shouldn't call me that." She raised the metal bar up over her head. "You won't ever call me that again, either. You're about to slip and hit your head on the tub grieving for your departed wife. The wife you've seen everywhere. Too bad, Jack. You really were the best lay I've ever had. Goodbye, Jack."

She went to bring the bar down on his head.

Then she stopped. Her eyes went wide and her mouth opened. Her whole body began to tremble.

Blood spurted out between her perfect white teeth.

Bracing his shoes against the side of the tub Jack sat up as best he could, still holding his broken hand. He stared in disbelief as Veronica slowly folded up to the floor of the bathroom, dead. The bar thumped to the floor and rattled away to a corner.

Behind where she'd been standing, Maria glared down at Jack. Her face was a horrible mask of hatred and violence. Her eyes held the flames of Hell themselves.

"Maria," he sputtered, still choking out water laced with soap bubbles. "Oh, honey. Oh, thank you. Help me, honey. Help me out. Thank you. Thank you so much."

She looked down at him for a long moment as he tried for the edge of the tub again. He didn't understand. Why wasn't she helping him? He was worth saving. He was an important man. A powerful man. He was the most important man in the world.

Surging forward, his dead wife's hands grasped him around his neck and together they fell into the bathtub. He tried to scream, but the water wouldn't let him.

ONE DARK PARTY

Frankie closed the trailer door and winced when it gave a loud click as it shut. She stood in the cold air in her denim shorts and her brother's old Van Halen t-shirt and listened. She could hear only the birds slowly waking up in the pale blue morning light. She half-expected to hear the familiar thunder of her daddy's voice to come through, demanding breakfast and coffee, but he hadn't seen eight in the morning since he lost his job five years ago, so she felt safe enough. She touched the five dollars in her pocket to make sure it was still there, then she headed towards the woods.

Happy Heavens was enormous as trailer parks went around here, but Frankie had it all mapped out it her head with the quietest routes to anywhere she'd want to go at any time of day or night. It helped that their two-tone rust bucket of a trailer was in the far back, near the woods, with no neighbors. If she needed to go to the store right now, she knew who would still be asleep and who would leave her alone if they happened to see her passing. She knew exactly how to avoid any assholes and do-gooders. It was a five-minute run; speed was important when daddy was out of beer. If she had a half-hour free from chores and had finished her latest library book then she could get to the playground in the suburb nearby in ten minutes without having to see anyone who knew her. They had fewer swings and only a pretty pathetic baby's slide there, but Happy Heavens' playground was where all the dealers hung out, so that was a no-go zone. Her daddy told her she was too old for swings at fourteen. She thought maybe that's why she still liked them, because he didn't.

Today, Frankie was headed to the east side of town, so she had to walk through the woods at the edge of the trailer park for a while to avoid a couple of the biggest assholes, then cut through for the last third of the park and come out onto the road safe and sound and unseen.

The circus was in town, and Frankie had never seen a circus.

Nothing much came to Waleska, Georgia, so she couldn't pass this up. She smiled to herself. She knew it would probably be closed, but she wanted to just see it, maybe even walk around a little.

If there are elephants there, she thought, I'm gonna flip out!

Frankie hopped the fence and landed with a crunch on the fallen leaves that covered the ground. She walked ten feet into the trees to be sure no-one could see her and to enjoy the sound of the birds. She lived with her headphones on, listening over and over to her brother's old punk rock mix tapes, but she enjoyed the sound of the real world when hardly anyone was awake in it.

A cracking sound ahead caught her attention, but she was too late to avoid being spotted.

"Motherfucker," a voice came, "I thought we talked about this?"

It was Heinrich. He was nearly twenty, balding before his time and only few cheeseburgers shy of a heart attack. He was dressed in army clothes and he gave a toothy grin. When Frankie saw his air rifle she froze.

"These aren't your woods," he said, looking confused, "are they?"

Frankie started walking backwards.

"In fact," he said, "I remember a chat we had where we discussed this, like, at length."

If Heinrich was here... she thought.

An arm grabbed her from behind and locked around her head tight.

"Get off me, you son of a bitch!" she shouted.

Heinrich was in hysterics, laughing his ass off. Frankie pushed her way free of the headlock and jumped back. It was Henry, Heinrich's younger brother. He was about half his brother's size, lengthwise and width wise, with a half-grown mustache and a lisp.

"Did you say something about mom?" Henry said, lisping his way through the S's.

Frankie ran back towards her trailer. She knew she could outrun both of them. "Fuck your mom!" she shouted, immediately disappointing herself, but they deserve it, she thought.

She could hear them stampeding through the leaves after her. When she was twenty yards ahead she turned sharply and tried to loop back past them. As she did, she felt a sharp sting in the side of her knee that buckled it and sent her tumbling to the ground. She screamed and looked up as Henry and Heinrich walked over.

"Shit," Heinrich said, laughing and holding up his air rifle, "I'm pretty good with this thing!"

Henry didn't laugh. Henry rarely laughed. He had the same half-scowl for all occasions.

"What the fuck did you say about our mom?" Henry said.

He kicked Frankie in the side, causing her to curl up like one of those bugs that she used to play with when she was a little girl; she was a human roly poly. Henry stood on her back and then sat down on top of her, pressing the air out of her lungs. He grabbed both of her arms and twisted them back as she cried out.

"Apologize!" Henry said.

"I'm sorry!" Frankie said.

Heinrich stood over her and pointed the air rifle at her head.

"Don't!" Frankie said. "Please!"

Heinrich laughed. "Hold her still," he said. He put his air rifle on his back and picked up a handful of dry leaves off the ground. He bent down as far as his belly would allow with the leaves in his hand and said, "Open up, bitch."

Frankie squirmed and tried to shake herself free in a blind panic. She hated dirt. She couldn't stand bugs. She wanted to die right there and then. More than anything in the world, she wanted to die immediately so she wouldn't have to do this. It wasn't normal to be this afraid of bugs and dirt, she knew that. She couldn't explain it. But she couldn't control it either. There was no reasoning with the fear. It overwhelmed her.

Heinrich shoved the leaves against her mouth, but she wouldn't open up.

"You scared?" Heinrich said. "Ha! She's scared of bugs, I guess! What a geek!"

Henry twisted her arms back more and when she screamed Heinrich shoved the leaves in.

Then, Henry laughed.

"Eat up, little squirrel!" Heinrich said, almost crying with laughter.

The leaves tasted foul and scratched the roof of Frankie's mouth. She convulsed violently to get free and spat them out, screaming and thrashing, and Henry got off, having had his fun and enjoying watching her frantic display.

"If we see you in here again," Henry said, "I'm gonna bring my daddy's gun. And that doesn't shoot pellets, you get me?"

Frankie stood and wiped the tears from her eyes and the dried bits of leaves from her mouth.

"You get me, little squirrel?" he said again.

She nodded, scowling

Heinrich cleared his throat and spat on Frankie's t-shirt. "Van Halen sucks," he said.

Frankie was shaking as she brushed her hair out of her eyes and wiped the dirt from her face. She took slow steps backwards away from them and in the direction of the circus. She turned and started walking, slower than before, limping a little, her face burning with shame.

"Ugly bitch!" Heinrich shouted after her.

He fired his air rifle in her direction again, hitting a nearby tree.

Frankie ran. The harder she ran and the farther away she got from Happy Heavens, the less she cried.

It was always the same.

Whether it was her daddy or any other asshole, Frankie always ended up running.

Frankie felt worthless and pathetic and alone. The anger would come later.

This is how it always was.

*

Waleska, Georgia, wasn't much to look at. There was very little in the way of redeeming features, as far as Frankie could see, other than it being smaller than most places and therefore having fewer people. The population had only in the last decade or so crept up over five thousand, thanks largely to the boom in the popularity of trailer parks after the economy died a death. The owner of Happy Heavens was making a killing, but there were few local businesses and therefore there was no real reason for anyone to be in town. This meant that mornings were quiet. You could walk down the main street and not see a single car. Frankie headed down past the auto repair shop where her daddy used to work, before the bad times. She went around the high school she rarely attended and cut through the football field to avoid seeing the intersection where a truck took away her mom and her older brother. A half-mile in she cut back onto the same road and saw the circus tent rising up over the trees ahead.

Frankie couldn't bring herself to smile again yet after the beating she took, but she was starting to put it to the back of her mind. For the time being, she had scolded herself for being pathetic, cursed herself seven ways from Sunday, and decided that it was OK because one day she would leave this place. She had decided the same thing a hundred times before, of course, but the promise still helped her to cope. She'd developed a knack for dealing with these kinds of beatings over the years. It was almost a skill.

The circus was pitched in a field with a red banner hung from the border fence. "Bakker Bros. World Famous Circus!" it said, showing a grinning clown face and a trapeze artist mid-jump. The big top tent was white with red stripes and as high as a three-story building. Frankie ran up to the gate and she spotted bumper cars, hoop games and popcorn stands. She couldn't see any people.

Frankie climbed over the gate and walked carefully up to the corner of a closed-up hot dog truck nearby. She peered around it. No alarms sounded and no dogs barked, so she decided to take a walk around.

The sky was brightening some now, and, though she wished she could see it at night all lit up, Frankie was captivated by the place. Most of Frankie's time was taken up by chores, but the rest she devoted to reading. She didn't like science fiction or horror or anything too old. She jumped from book to book as fast as she could, and she loved more than anything to read about faraway places – *real* places – and imagine that one day she could visit them. She had read about circuses, seen them on TV when she was allowed to watch, and visiting one had made it onto her mental list of things she'd do once she was free, when she had her own place - a house, not a trailer - and her own money and no-one to tell her what to do. Frankie used to consider running away all the time, crafting elaborate plans and staring at maps, but now her plans had been replaced with a simple deep longing to be somewhere else. She didn't want to get her hopes up with place names and deadlines. Once, she really tried to leave. She took her school backpack, filled it with canned food, stole twenty bucks from her daddy, and bought a bus ticket. She was found three towns over on the same day and beaten so hard she ended up in the infirmary. She was twelve years old. Since then, she didn't make real plans. Instead, she spent her days running away in small ways, through her route maps of the trailer park, through staying in her room and pretending to go to sleep earlier than she really did, and through her books and tapes.

Reality, for Frankie, meant chores and shouting and punches and cruel names and no friends, so she shut out as much of it as she could.

A haunted house caught Frankie's eye with wooden cut-out ghosts and a deep-sea diver that looked just like the one in *Scooby Doo*. She was easily tall enough to get in, but it was shut, the cars covered with plastic sheets. The cars were built for two people, she noticed. She wondered what it would be like to be able to notice something like that without feeling sad.

"You work here?" a voice came.

Frankie raised her eyebrows and looked to see an Indian man staring at her with a look of confusion. He was tall and dark-skinned with long, black hair and he wore jeans and an Atari t-shirt. He looked about thirty years old and his accent was pure California. He had tattoos on his arms, Frankie noticed, but they were just big, black blotches, as if they were once normal tattoos that had now been filled in and covered up. They looked like leopard spots.

Frankie fidgeted with her hands a second and nodded.

"What do you do?" the man asked.

"I - uh..." Frankie started. Behind the Indian man she saw a midget walking past. He looked like the clown on the banner, but he was wearing shorts and t-shirt and carrying a Chihuahua. He looked at Frankie and nodded good morning.

"I'm..." she tried again.

"You can't be here," the Indian man said. "If the boss catches you, he'll lose his shit."

"What do you do here?" Frankie said. "I've never been to a circus."

"You can't be here, kid," he said. "Come on."

The Indian man walked over and put his hand on her back to usher her back towards the gate. When Frankie flinched away from his slight touch, he stopped and his face softened as he looked at her. Frankie didn't know what he was looking at, but she didn't like to be touched. She didn't like people looking at her.

I just want to see the goddamn elephants, she thought, her stomach turning with disappointment.

The combined fear and hurt and hope made Frankie feel sick. And it made her look scared.

"I tell you what," the Indian man said, "what if I could get you some tickets for tonight's show?"

"I can't," she said. "I have things to do. Daddy would be mad."

The Indian man looked like he was becoming impatient or angry, Frankie couldn't tell which. He looked all around to see if anyone was watching, then, seeing no-one, he lightened up.

"Alright," he said, putting on a smile. "How about a tour? I don't think the boss is around, so it should be alright."

Frankie's eyes lit up. "Do you have elephants?"

The Indian man laughed. "We have one, yeah. You want to meet her?"

Frankie nodded, feeling joyful tears hit her eyes at the very thought of it.

"What's your name?" he asked.

"Frankie," she said.

"Francesca?"

Her mom used to call her Francesca.

"I'm sorry," he said. "Frankie, it is. My name's Tommy."

"Tommy?"

"Tommy Hawk," he said with a smile. "Let's go this way."

They started walking past the big top tent.

He whispered, "It's not really, but that's what the posters say. My real name's Teddy."

Frankie smiled. That was a much better name, she thought. "Where are you from?" she asked.

"I'm from LA originally."

"No, I mean... Um..."

"Oh," Teddy laughed. "I'm Cheyenne through and through."

"There was a boy in school was a... uh..."

"You can say Indian," Teddy said. "It's not a dirty word. What tribe was he from?"

"He was a Cheyenne, too," she said.

"Then that's what call him, a Cheyenne. Not many of us left. Here we are."

They'd arrived at a smaller tent. It wasn't designed for visitors and looked more like a military tent. A sign outside said, simply, "Animals".

"Is there really an elephant in there?" Frankie asked. "You're not shitting me?"

Teddy laughed. "No shit, Frankie."

The tent was empty but for two large cages and buckets of some kind of animal feed. The first cage was empty. Teddy looked shocked for a second and whispered, "Oh, God, no! The tiger's escaped!"

"Shut up," Frankie said, grinning. "I'm not an idiot."

"No, you're not," Teddy said with a nod. "Frankie, meet Tabitha."

Tabitha was gray and wrinkled with pock-marked skin and small course hairs on her head. She was the size of a van. Her trunk touched the ground and was curled up slightly. Her tail flicked here and there. She was very still otherwise, only moving her head slightly when she saw her visitors. Frankie ran up to the cage and put her hands on the bars.

"She's beautiful!" Frankie said with a wide grin. "Come here, girl."

The elephant moved back a little. Its eyes, old and tired around the outside but vivid and alive within, watched Frankie warily. Tabitha's enormous ears twitched as a fly buzzed around her head.

"How old is she?" Frankie asked.

"She's ten, I think," Teddy said.

"Is that old?"

"She's still a baby. Elephants can live until they're sixty, you know?"

Frankie was impressed. She smiled and tried again to reach out to touch Tabitha, but Tabitha backed away. Something about her troubled Frankie. In the twitches of her ears, the light flap of her tail and the shifting of her great weight on her feet, Tabitha looked nervous. Frankie noticed her cage was only somewhat bigger than the elephant herself, and food was piled on the ground and left uneaten.

Teddy noticed Frankie's smile starting to fade.

"She's, uh, very friendly usually," Teddy said. "She's scared of new people, I guess."

Frankie drew her hand out. "Does she come out of the cage much?"

"Only for shows," Teddy said, grimacing a little.

Tabitha turned in her cage to face away from them.

"We better leave her rest," Teddy said.

Frankie noticed whip marks on the elephant's back.

Teddy caught her looking at them and started walking away from the cage, expecting Frankie to follow. "Come on," he said. "You want to see where I work?"

Frankie looked at Tabitha a little longer. Tabitha didn't look back.

Maybe she doesn't like to be looked at or touched either, Frankie thought.

*

Teddy worked out of a small, brightly colored gypsy caravan.

"Cheyennes don't live in these, do they?" Frankie said.

"No," Teddy said, "but it's all the same to the whites who run this place. They don't think anyone can tell the difference."

Inside was decorated with clay and wooden ornaments of owls, deer and wolves, and feathers hung on strings from the roof. A compartment at the back, behind a curtain, had just enough room for a small refrigerator, a television set, an old Nintendo and a bunk.

"What do you do?" Frankie asked.

"Tattoos," Teddy said. "Mostly temporary tattoos of Indian designs. Sometimes I have to branch out into face-painting for the kids to make a little more money. I can do real tattoos, though. I taught myself a long time ago. I got pretty good at it."

"Were you in prison?" Frankie played with a feather that was laid on a table in the middle. Teddy sat down.

"I was," Teddy said, going into the back. "I'm not so scary, though."

"I know," Frankie said.

"Here," Teddy said, handing her a soda pop. "You eaten anything today?"

Frankie's face turned red. "Leaves," she said. She sat down and held the feather in her hand. She looked at it so she wouldn't have to look at Teddy. He was a do-gooder, she could see that now. The trailer park was full of them. A hundred times Frankie had walked around with a black eye or cigarette burns on her arms and people would stop her and say how terrible it all was, but none of them would ever do anything for her. They thought saying was enough, but it wasn't.

She didn't want words.

"Your daddy make you do that?" Teddy said.

Frankie shook her head. Teddy handed her a Twinkie and she opened it up, smiling a sad thank you.

"Hey," Teddy said, "how about I give you a tattoo? A little one? I can do a little elephant for you."

"My daddy wouldn't like that."

"Just a temporary one. I can do it at the top of your arm there, where he wouldn't see."

Frankie's hands shook as she nibbled her Twinkie. "He'd see," she said, "wherever it was."

Teddy went into the back and came back with a beer for himself, opening it with his teeth and spitting the bottle cap out on the floor. As he had his back turned, Frankie wolfed down the Twinkie. She didn't like people to see her eat. Teddy sat and drank - he appeared changed in some undefinable way - and Frankie had some of her soda. Frankie saw that Teddy's hand was shaking a little, too.

"Can I tell you a story?" Teddy said.

"Sure, I don't mind," Frankie said.

"A long time ago - I'm talking about the 1800s, now - there was a village of Cheyenne people and some others down in Colorado. They used to have a great big piece of land, until, one day, someone struck gold nearby. Then, the government came on down and they took that land away from my people. Some of my people agreed. They signed contracts they couldn't read, took gifts, and then they found themselves cooped up with nowhere to go, like Tabitha back there. After a while, some of the Cheyenne, they didn't like this, so they started to get angry. They started leaving the cage that had been made for them, riding and hunting in the old lands they used to own."

"Like in movies?" Frankie said.

"Just like in the movies, riding and shooting guns and arrows with their shirts off and all that great stuff. Then there came the war, and lots of soldiers came with it. And to the white men, my people weren't worth a damn. All they could see was land, lots of it, which my people had the nerve to live on. There was a chief at this village, he'd been to the White House, you know? The president himself had given him an American flag. And he was so proud, this chief. He'd raise that flag every day over the village. And when he heard that soldiers had been going around the country, murdering his people? He said, 'No. This will not happen to us. We are Americans.' Even when the soldiers rolled up on his village, he just raised that flag. The men were all out hunting that day, leaving only women, kids and the old folks. And this chief gathered everyone up and said, 'If you stand under this flag, nothing bad will happen to you.' So they did. Have you heard about this in school?"

Frankie shook her head.

"You won't. The white men call it The Battle of Sand Creek. My people had a different name for it: The Sand Creek Massacre. Nearly a thousand soldiers rode in there and murdered a hundred and fifty, two hundred people - women, children, old folks. And they murdered them good, let me tell you. Even the babies. They took trophies so they could show off to their friends back home: ears, noses; they'd even skin the tattoo off someone as a keepsake."

Frankie was starting to feel a little sick.

Teddy nodded. "Yep," he said. "My daddy used to tell me all about this stuff. 'That's how the white man's world works,' he'd say. Because, you see, Frankie, white men take and take and take and they convince you that it's for the best. They take everything you have, and they get you so scared and so beaten down that eventually you have to convince yourself that you're happy with what you got, because otherwise what's the point in living?"

Frankie put the feather down on the table. Teddy swigged his beer and took a deep breath, trying not to look angry, but Frankie could still see it.

"Let me give you a tattoo," Teddy said, putting down his bottle. "A real one."

Frankie swallowed. She didn't want to say no to him when he looked that upset.

"I have some special ink," he said. He leaned in and lowered his voice. "People like those who you met today, people like your daddy, they don't give you respect. They don't treat you like a human being, right? Growing up Cheyenne, I know all about that. It nearly took my life, but then I got myself an education, a dark education, you get me?"

Frankie was quiet. She hugged her arm with her hand and her leg was shaking.

"You can't be afraid your whole life, Frankie," Teddy said. "Let me help you. No-one will ever touch you again, I promise you that."

Frankie wanted to say yes.

"There are forces in this world that men like that haven't even *dreamed* of."

Frankie wanted to say yes. Teddy walked into his bedroom compartment and pulled up the carpet in the corner. Underneath, in a small, dark gap, was a wooden box with horses carved into it. Teddy brought it back and laid it on the table.

"This isn't Cheyenne stuff I'm talking about here. This isn't some kind of Indian magic bullshit," he said. "This is the real deal. The ink that's in this box will give you all the help you'll ever need. You won't have to ask for it, it'll just come. This ink will connect you with the earth itself. This is dark shit. This is low magic. The dark and the low creatures, they'll become your friends. You'll never have to be afraid of anyone. You'll never had to run from anything ever again."

Frankie wanted to say yes. "Are you tricking me?" she said.

Teddy took her hand and looked her in the eye. She tried to pull her hand back at first but then she looked up at him. She could see in his eyes a lifetime's worth of anger, but also compassion. "I don't want your money, Frankie. People like you and me," he said, "we have to look out for one another."

"OK," Frankie said. "Do it."

Teddy nodded. He opened the box. Inside was an ink bottle, a series of different sized needles and a small wooden stick.

"The design is very specific," Teddy said.

"It's not an elephant, is it?" Frankie said.

"No. Roll up your sleeve."

"What is it?"

Frankie turned up the sleeve of her baggy t-shirt. Underneath was a large, sore bruise. Teddy clenched his fist when he saw it. He looked at her and said, "It's a snake."

*

Frankie's tattoo burned her skin as she jumped over the fence and got back on the road home. She had tears in her eyes and a little blood was seeping out from under the bandage. Walking back in the full light of day, Frankie felt like she had emerged from a dream in which she'd made a horrible mistake. She took the long path back through the trailer park which stayed well clear of Henry and Heinrich's trailer and out of the woods. When she got home it was ten o' clock and she knew her daddy would be waking up soon. The trailer, once painted green and white but now mostly green with mold and brown with weathering, was little bigger than Tabitha's cage.

The door closed behind her and she stopped and held her breath for a moment, listening for signs that her daddy was awake. There was nothing. Frankie went into the tiny bathroom, no bigger than an airplane bathroom, she imagined, and she rolled up her sleeve. Unpeeling the bandage from the bottom, Frankie got her first look at the design. The ink was a deep black and spots of blood surrounded it. The long, thick snake was wrapped around the top of her arm, its head resting just under her shoulder. The snake's scales were intricate patterns that looked like words in a long-forgotten language. It didn't look like any Indian drawing she'd ever seen. The snake was angular and almost mathematical-looking.

"Cool," she whispered, but she couldn't shake the sickness in her stomach, the knowledge of what her daddy would do if he saw it.

Wiping away the blood, Frankie pulled on a long-sleeve t-shirt and began tidying up the trailer ready for her daddy. When a low moan sounded from the bedroom, Frankie went in to begin their daily routine. Her daddy's legs weren't what they were before the crash. It was a long time since he wrapped the car around a tree and killed his wife and son. Somehow, the physical pain remained. It would come and go. Sometimes it was a dull ache that caused him to be irritable, other times it was a sharp agony which meant he couldn't walk more than a few steps, sending him to the bottle, to shouting, to violence.

Opening her daddy's bedroom door, Frankie saw him sat on the edge of his bed with his head in his hands.

Today is a bad day, she thought.

"What are you lookin' at?" he said, without turning his head. "I can hear you sneaking around from a mile away."

'Want some breakfast?" Frankie said.

Her daddy grunted. Frankie went to prepare bacon and eggs. He followed her through, leaning on the walls and on the kitchen units, groaning in pain. A small patch of wetness on Frankie's arm started to nag at her attention.

It's still bleeding, she thought.

She tried to turn herself away from her daddy at every opportunity as he shuffled by and slumped onto the sofa chair beside the dining table. His face was drawn and gray beneath permanent stubble and the dark eyes and red nose of a habitual drunk. As Frankie lay his breakfast on the table in front of him, his half-glazed eyes fell on her shoulder. On seeing his daughter bleeding, his first words were, "I didn't do that."

Frankie said nothing. She took out a single Pop Tart for herself and jumped up and sat on the counter to nibble at it.

"What you do?" her daddy said.

"I just cut myself on a branch in the woods," she said, trying to sound relaxed as every muscle in her body tensed. "It's nothin'."

Through a mouthful of bacon, her daddy said, "I decide what's nothin'. Come here."

"It's OK," she said, forcing a smile. "I'm OK."

"I ain't askin' if you're OK," he said. "I'm asking what you done to your goddamn arm."

Frankie sat and took a small bite of her breakfast. She was shutting down. Her eyes fixed on a spot on the wall opposite. Her legs stopped swinging. She didn't even swallow her breakfast, rather, she chewed it gently as if stuck in a loop. She let herself enter the loop automatically. Trouble would either begin or go away and all she could do was wait and see.

"Come over here, right now," her daddy said.

Trouble had begun.

"What the hell have you been doing around here?" he said. He stood.

"It's nothin," Frankie said, the loop dissolving under the pressure. "I got beat up," she said quickly.

Her daddy scowled at her. "Who?" he said.

"It doesn't-"

"If you tell me one more time what does or doesn't matter in my own house then you can get out and never come back."

"It was Henry and Heinrich," she said. "Those guys are assholes."

"Did you hit them first?" he said.

"No! I told you, they're assholes. They always hit me!"

"You musta done something," her daddy said, pointing. "I know their mom pretty good. She's a good friend of mine. You better go over there right now and apologize."

Frankie felt as if she'd been hit in the stomach, again.

"Apologize for what?"

"You better get your skinny ass over there right now and tell them you're sorry for whatever you did or I'm gonna make you sorry."

Her daddy came around the table and stood right in front of her. He snatched her Pop Tart from her and threw it to the floor. Frankie looked at her shoes.

"You hearing me, girl?" her daddy said. "I have had just about enough of your shit."

"I didn't do anything," she mumbled.

"What?"

"I didn't do *nothing*," she said.

"Lift up your face," her daddy said. "Lift it up. Look at me."

Frankie slowly lifted her head to look at her daddy. As she got high enough to look up into his eyes, his open hand slapped across Frankie's face with a clack. She turned and put her face in her hands. Through her own sobs she could hear him.

"I say what you've done around here," her daddy said. "I'm not having the whole park thinking I'm keeping a troublemaker."

He grabbed her arm and yanked her down to the floor. She hit hard and didn't want to get back up. From her position on the floor she could see underneath the sofa, into the trailer's hidden places. Something was moving in the dark, she thought. Looking closer, ignoring her daddy's insults, she could see that the darkness was alive.

Everything was moving in there.

The darkness had a hundred legs and a hundred eyes. Her daddy pulled her to her feet and grabbed a walking crutch and threw her out the trailer door.

"We're going visiting, you little shit," he said.

*

Henry and Heinrich's trailer was twice as long as Frankie's and built into a ramshackle L-shape with an extension crafted from scrap wood and plastic sheets which acted as a tool shed and (not very) secret meth lab. Her daddy stumbled as best he could through the mud behind Frankie, hurling curses at her the whole way. Frankie had stopped proclaiming her innocence. She had resigned herself to humiliation.

But something inside her was ready.

Frankie felt a kind of stillness. She had felt acceptance before. She had taken the beatings and everything else and put it to the back of her mind. This wasn't the same. This acceptance felt different. Her face burned red, but not with shame. For the first time, she was angry on schedule, as needed, and she felt something of a purpose rising within her.

The darkness in the trailer had given her a glimmer of how the world really is - a disgusting, ferocious hole into which the human race had fallen - and it had given her a glimpse of what she could be in this world. The darkness was coming to her, she was convinced of that.

As she thought about it, her pace quickened to the point where her daddy had to slow her down. She could feel the darkness following her. The long grass moved in her wake. The leaves rustled. Tiny legs silently followed. Tiny eyes watched. Frankie felt them. She could feel the darkness at her back and it gave her strength. Her calmness now was not the silence of defeat. It was the calm before the storm.

"Henry!" her daddy shouted in an amused tone as they approached. "Heinrich! Get out here, you sorry sons of bitches."

Frankie stopped when she saw them emerge from their trailer, looking half-confused and full-drunk. Henry was in a bathrobe. Heinrich wore only dirty underpants, but he was carrying a shotgun.

"What you want, old man?" Henry shouted.

Frankie stood frozen to the spot, but her daddy hit her with his walking crutch and pointed her towards to the trailer. Frankie could feel a pressure building in her head. She could hear a low ringing noise which was becoming more and more intolerable. The darkness was with her and she was fighting the urge to go back to her room to read her books, to pretend her life was bearable, to pretend her daddy still loved her deep down and that the world had something it was going to offer her one day, that she had a future. Every time her daddy hit her and poked her with the crutch, it chipped away at that idea of a future. It made it harder for Frankie to refuse the darkness.

"Your mom home, boys?" Frankie's daddy said. "Me and Frankie here need to talk with her. With you, too."

The brothers looked at one another with sly smiles.

"Come on in," Henry said.

Frankie had been taken to other trailers before. The men who lived in them, Frankie's routes through the park took her nowhere near them. She could see where this night was headed and she was almost relieved. What they were doing, for Frankie, made her thoughts OK. What they had planned, it justified the onset of the darkness that nipped at her heels. She felt like she could give herself to the dark and low creatures of the world completely. She would let them take what they wanted of these men, so that no man would ever take anything of her again.

She didn't know what the darkness had in store, but it felt big, final.

The interior of the trailer looked like an indoor junkyard and smelled like a cow shed. Oily car parts covered the table, beer cans covered the floor, decade-old pornographic magazine pin-ups decorated the walls and a skinned and treated deer hung headless over the kitchen sink. Frankie stepped inside and Heinrich was directly behind her. She could feel his breath on the back of her neck as he giggled.

Behind the giggling and the small talk and the blaring television which called the plays on a college football game, Frankie could hear a whispering and a sneaking and a crawling. A dark cloud was descending upon the trailer as these men laughed and joked and scratched their crotches and spat on their own floor. Their mother was in the master bedroom. Frankie was led in by her daddy. The woman was sick and lying under a thin, dirty green sheet tucked under her chin, like a gray turtle stuck on its back and doomed to die. At first glance, Frankie thought she was dead, but then she tried to speak. It was German. It was mumbled. It barely qualified as words.

"Looking good, Eva," Frankie's daddy said, standing beside Frankie, cornering her next to the living corpse, the dying turtle. Henry stood at the foot of the bed, watching with his beady eyes. Heinrich's huge frame blocked the doorway. "I hate to bother you," Frankie's daddy said, "but I understand there's been some trouble."

Eva said something else that wasn't words, her ashen face barely moving.

Frankie's daddy looked at Henry.

"She says Frankie is a bitch," Henry said without a hint of a smile. Heinrich chuckled.

"I'm real sorry," Frankie's daddy said. "Truly, I am. I don't know what to do with the girl."

Eva stared at the ceiling, passive, distant. She coughed and speckles of phlegm jumped out of her mouth and onto her face.

"Momma says something should be done," Henry said.

Frankie's fist balled up. She stared a hole through the wall almost, looking straight ahead. Her jaws locked together and the pressure was so hard she thought her teeth might bend and break. Her eyes were stinging with tears. She didn't want anything to happen, but she could feel the pressure building in her head. One of two bad things was about to happen, she knew. It would either be the old bad thing - the thing that had haunted her sleep, which she had spent her waking hours trying to escape from both physically and mentally - or it would be some kind of new bad thing.

"How much money you boys got between you?" Frankie's daddy asked.

They looked Frankie over. Henry said, "We got enough."

Teddy's words returned to Frankie in a loop: "They take and take and take and take and take." His words echoed in her head. "They take everything you have, and they get you so scared and so beaten down that eventually you have to convince yourself that you're happy with what you got, because otherwise what's the point in living?"

Her daddy grabbed her arm and shoved her out past Henry and Heinrich and into the other bedroom. The two brothers were laughing. Tears ran down Frankie's face, but she slowed down her actions, made herself aware of her surroundings. There was one dirty window, broken in one corner and too grimy to let much light through. Stacks of detective and pornographic magazines filled much of the room. Cobwebs dangled from the corners.

"You don't mind if I pull up a chair?" Frankie's daddy said.

Teddy's words returned to Frankie: "That's how the white man's world works."

"Lie on the bed," Henry said.

Frankie sat on the edge of the bed. Her tattoo was a burning pain and a constant reminder of the power she had been promised by Teddy, a power that she could feel growing as the world grew dimmer.

"What the hell is that?" Heinrich said. "The little squirrel got a tattoo?"

He lifted up her sleeve and tore off the bandage. Frankie looked at it. The snake design looked to her to be perfect. It was like looking at the blueprints of a well-designed building, she thought. It had stopped bleeding. It didn't even look sore any more. It had healed.

It looked as though it had always been there.

"What?!" her daddy stood up and grabbed her arm from the other side of the bed and yanked her over to him, almost pulling her arm out of her socket. "When the hell did you get this shit? What is that? Is that a snake?!"

He punched her in the back of the head and she curled up in a ball. Her daddy's fury made Henry and Heinrich take a step back.

"Are you trying to make me look bad?!" her daddy shouted as he punched her again.

Frankie lay on the bed curled into a ball with her hands covering her head and her knees drawn up to her chest. She closed her eyes and tried to place her mind elsewhere as another punch landed on her back. The punches stopped for a moment as her daddy removed his belt and wrapped the end of it around his hand. The first strike cracked against her back and opened up her skin and her eyes bolted open. She screamed involuntarily, but she wouldn't beg. There had been a shift in her mind: I will either die, she thought, or this will never happen again. The pressure in her mind was still building.

Her daddy grabbed her and pulled her off the bed, choking her and slamming her back against the wardrobe. Frankie looked deep into her daddy's eyes. He looked beyond her, maybe to a life without her, maybe to nothing, and tightened his grip on her throat.

The bedroom was growing darker, as though the day had already retired and night had begun. When Frankie looked beyond her daddy to the dirty window, it looked black outside.

The blackness shifted, she noticed. It wasn't night at all. Something was covering the window.

Then they entered the trailer.

Creatures poured in like black liquid through a broken section of the window and seeped up through the broken floorboards as if the trailer was suddenly drowned in a lake of tar.

"What the hell?!" Heinrich shouted as he was swarmed in insects and spiders.

Frankie was suffocating under her daddy's grip. Her vision was failing. Her muscles were becoming limp. Her hearing was becoming distorted, as if she was being submerged. But the whispering she had heard earlier was back.

It was a million small voices, all saying her name. She opened her eyes and tried to speak to them. Though she didn't have the strength to speak, they heard her cries.

The black tar that was filling the trailer started to break off into thousands of little shapes. There were spiders of a hundred varieties – house spiders, money spiders, daddy long legs – and a plethora of insects – black beetles, grasshoppers, cockroaches. A carpet of small snakes and large centipedes writhed around their feet and rose, wrapping themselves around the men. Frankie's fear overpowered her anger and she felt only joy at seeing them.

Frankie's daddy dropped her and she fell to the floor with her back to the wall as he tried in vain to brush off hundreds of insects that were crawling up his legs and into his clothes. He started screaming as he felt their legs tickling his body all over and began hitting himself to squash them.

"What the hell is going on?!" he screamed.

Frankie covered her mouth in shock.

"Get 'em off me!" Heinrich shouted, waving his arms and his shotgun all around in a blind panic. "Get 'em off me!"

"Stand-" Henry began, reaching for his brother, before a deafening blast of the shotgun cut Henry's sentence off along with the top half of his skull which exploded against the wall as Heinrich's finger brushed the trigger.

"Oh, God!" Heinrich shouted as Henry's corpse dropped into the tide of small insects. Heinrich lifted his gun and fired into a gap in the floorboards where long, brown swamp snakes were swarming through. "You little bastards!" he shouted. He began screaming as they lunged and bit into his legs and crotch.

After a few moments of shock, Frankie, untouched by the insects and the snakes, removed her hand from her mouth to reveal a smile. She stood up.

Heinrich fell to the floor next to the half-headless corpse of his brother. He dropped the shotgun and started writhing in agony and flapping his arms as he was bitten by a hundred snakes and stung by a thousand tiny spider bites. There were no poisonous creatures, for that's the way Frankie wanted it. Heinrich screamed and his eyes locked on Frankie as inch-by-inch his body was nipped away and his blood merged with the black tide of the dark and low creatures.

"Help me!" he shouted to Frankie. "Do something!"

Frankie waved both hands as if conducting an orchestra and the insects and the snakes scattered away from Heinrich, parting and exposing his shredded flesh. Heinrich looked around in horror as the insects obeyed Frankie. She swirled her right hand and those to her right scurried in a spiral motion up and across the wall. Frankie laughed. Her daddy looked up at her in horror from his position on his knees on the floor as he fought off cockroaches and dragged them out of his mouth and covered his nose.

"I am doing something," Frankie said.

She looked at Heinrich and stopped smiling.

"I'm not afraid of you," she said.

She brought her hands together in a clap and the insects and the spiders and the snakes came together in a wave from either side which engulfed Heinrich. He screamed with a mouth filled with centipedes until a long green-and-brown striped snake slithered out of the pool of blood on the floor and curled around Heinrich's neck and pressed its head into his mouth. Heinrich pulled at the snake, but it was too slippery to hold. Its tail wriggled back and forth in time with horrific choking noises from Heinrich as the snake tunneled its way deep into his throat and down into his chest. Heinrich's face turned blue as the tail of the snake disappeared down his mouth and the house spiders followed. He screamed silently, crunching spiders between his teeth as he gasped for air that wouldn't come. He grabbed his face in agony and tore at his skin with his nails, despairing in his final moments, ripping chunks from himself until at last he stopped moving but for the pulsating of his stomach where the snake and the spiders and the centipedes were squirming within him.

Frankie's daddy had found respite as the creatures swarmed over Heinrich and he looked back to his daughter with bloody tears in his eyes, his face red with small bites, his legs bleeding with larger ones.

"I'm-" he stuttered, looking at her, "I'm your daddy. You don't got no-one else."

Frankie said nothing.

"I love you, Frankie," her daddy said, raising his hands to her to plead. "You're my girl."

Frankie felt her insides turn to jelly and her knees begin to give underneath her. It was everything she had always wanted to hear. One kind word, she thought. I would've taken one kind word from this man and I would've been happy.

How wrong I was, she thought.

"You're my girl," her daddy said.

"I'm not your girl!" Frankie screamed. "I'm not your anything!"

Frankie's daddy jumped to his feet and pushed Frankie aside, slamming her head into the wall, as he made for the door. Holding her head, Frankie followed. The snakes zig-zagged over the bloodied carpet and into the hallway after her daddy where they leaped up at his legs and tore chunks from his ankles, sending him sprawling on his face into the lounge area. Standing over him, Frankie moved the creatures aside with a swoop of her hand.

Her daddy turned and looked up at her. "Please!" he screamed.

Frankie moved her fingers thinking of what to bring forth, and Georgia's most dangerous of the darkest and lowest creatures presented themselves, pushing through the black tide and encircling her daddy.

First came the snakes: the dusty-colored rattlesnakes; the green cottonmouths; the deadly copperheads. They surrounded her daddy. Then came the spiders and the scorpions: the glistening black widows, as big as a human hand; the small-bodied and almost translucent brown recluses; the chunky, brown devil scorpions. They crawled into the center of the circle made by the snakes and attached themselves to her daddy's body, crawling up his pants and down his sleeves and clinging to his screaming, white face. As the pincers closed around his skin and the scorpion's daggers penetrated his body, her daddy begged for his life in garbled, half-formed words as his bloodstream was overcome with poison that burned him from the inside out. When the snakes began to strike, they went for his face and genitals, popping his testicles and one of his eyeballs. Frankie raised her hands once more and the floorboards cracked and snapped upwards as she summoned the oldest of the low creatures. Three grinning alligators emerged from the darkness under the floorboards, pulling themselves through with small, powerful arms and propelling themselves with slashes of their long, thick tails. When her daddy saw the alligators, he emitted a single scream that lasted from the moment they arrived to the moment of his death. His scream was distorted and broken off by the jaws of the alligators around his head and body as they span and thrashed and broke every bone in his body, but it returned spasmodically as his body returned to something approaching its normal position for a split-second in between being twisted and pulverized by rows upon rows of razor-sharp teeth.

Frankie's father and his attackers became a nightmarish biomass on the floor, a thrashing, writhing, screaming and roaring collective of nature and humanity.

Within moments, the beating heart of the biomass, Frankie's horrified, tortured father, stopped moving. The creatures continued their feast and Frankie sat on the floor amidst them.

She was no longer afraid of any creature the earth could produce.

She tucked her knees up to her chest and rested her chin on her folded arms. She closed her eyes and wished for nothing further other than to disappear forever. She could feel it happening as she rested. A silk blanket was engulfing her, growing around her as the spiders worked to produce for her a cocoon. She opened her eyes and the darkness was complete. She was wrapped from head-to-toe in spider-webs. Rolling onto her side, she began to cry.

No library books could stop it.

No trips to the playground could distract her from it.

No mix-tapes could shut out her thoughts.

She was no longer afraid of any creature the earth could produce, apart from one – men – and she no longer wanted to live in place with such creatures.

The crocodiles and the snakes and the spiders and the scorpions worked as one and Frankie felt herself being pulled away from the world in her cocoon. Out of the trailer and into the woods and off to the wild nothing beyond.

She didn't know where they were dragging her. Frankie knew there was no place good to go to on this Earth.

Maybe they'll take me below it, she thought, where my mom is.

Maybe down there is better.

The End.

www.ingramcontent.com/pod-product-compliance
Lightning Source LLC
Chambersburg PA
CBHW022006120726
47992CB00001B/438